ShortCuts

A story about Choices and Consequences

By

T. L. Criswell

ISBN: 978-1-0902-5486-3

ShortCuts

What readers are saying about T.L. Criswell

Peace on That “A historically detailed, emotionally rich story of three generations of men dealing with and sometimes evading their duties to one another.

~Kirkus Reviews

A great read because there was a balance of joy and pain, but the lows never leave you hopeless. Tears of laughter or sorrow are just a page turn away.

~JJ Braden Paper back pushers

Peace on That “T.L. Criswell has given us full throttle of story telling and has taken readers on a historical ride of generational honor, dishonor, pride and loyalty”

~Vnae Amazon review

The Peacemaker “Criswell's literary debut is the best young adult offering of the decade! This writer takes us through the emotional progression of young Jayson Jackson as he emerges from juvenile delinquency to societal responsibility delivering a tumultuous hard knock that propelled the transition. This book will bring you to tears as you share with Jayson the passions of the guilt that will forever be a part of his life. Kudos to Criswell for such a thought provoking contribution to our young readers!”

~YA Librarian

"In a world where reading is often undervalued, ***The Peacemaker***, gives young readers material they can relate to and enjoy, simultaneously. The Peacemaker is realistic fiction that mirrors the lives of many young adults living in urban cities. I believe the story will spark a love for reading for some, and stoke the flames for those who already have an appreciation for literature. The Peacemaker definitely has classic potential."

~S.F. Hardy, Children/YA Librarian

The Peacemaker "This book truly spoke to these students, as it's both gritty and raw, while at the same time it's heartwarming and full of life. Her character development pulls you right in at the very beginning, and keeps you engaged through out the entire book. I highly recommend this book for middle and high schools, truly a great read,"

~ Barbara Jo Hawkins Detroit Librarian

"Sister Parker is a short but powerful read of challenges, lessons and blessings that's sure to touch your heart. BRAVO!"

~Ebony EyeCU Reading

"Sister Parker is a revelation. Soul quenching. The Emperor has no clothes."

~B. Smith

Note from the Author

Long before my hands touch a keyboard to pen a story; that story is formulated and crafted inside of my head.

This particular story, "ShortCuts" has lived inside of me for years. It wouldn't come into fruition until March of 2018 when I accepted a short story challenge from Ebony Evans of "EyeCU reading book club." She posted the topic "Mistaken Identity" at midnight, and each participant had 24 hours to create an original story on that topic.

After countless hours of anxiety, a few cups of coffee, and a bout of writers' block, I met the challenge and formulated a 2k-word short story titled "Mistaken Identity."

"Mistaken Identity" would become the building blocks for "Shortcuts;" an expanded, more in-depth version of this original story.

I want to send out a huge thank you to "Ebony Evans" and "EyeCU Reading" book club. You motivate, and inspire us all *"to keep pushing that pen."*

I am forever grateful,
T.L Criswell

Thank You

Writing a book is no easy task. It takes lots of patience, dedication, hard work and a team of enthusiastic people. I appreciate you all, and I just can't thank you enough.

I want to send out a thank you to my wonderful, supportive, husband James Criswell and my son Mehki Criswell.

Thank you to my mentor, adviser, producer and dear friend Ben C. Smith. I could not have written this novel without you.

Thank you to my beautiful and creative aunt Brenda Franklin.

Thank you "Paperback Pushers," for your assistance. Ms. Jymayaka Braden you captured the story so well. You rock!

Thank-you to my test readers and supporting staff: My mother, Jeanette Kirkland, my sister, Yvette Brown, my sister-in-law, Annette Rainer, my God daughter, Taylor Lewis, Arnika Davis, Tawanna Crumpton, Tijuana Clowney, Vincent Bennett, Teresa Horn, Valerie Bostic, Jymyaka Braden and Turura Crawford.

I want to give special thanks to some of my young readers, my son Mehki Criswell, my nephew Damon Terrelle, Essence Evans, Nadia Brown and Kennedy Donald.

I would also like to thank Stephanie Fazekas-hardy, Lurine Carter, and Rhena Deshawn from Detroit Public Library and Detroit Public school system for embracing my work.

A Special thank you to some of my biggest supporters, my brother-in-law DeWarren Criswell, Ricky McDaniel, Nancy Collins, Sharon Mathis, and Heather Perryman.

A Special thanks to all the book clubs that have supported my work, EyeCU reading book club, Brownstone book club, Something New Book Club, as well as Paperback Pushers.

And finally I would like to send a special thank you to each and every reader.

Peace and love,
T.L. Criswell

This book is dedicated to my beautiful mother,
Jeanette Kirkland.

Thank you for never giving up on
“little” Tiffany Parker.
Always your baby girl,
~T.L. Criswell~

Contents

Note from the Author vii

Thank You ix

The Butterflies xv

Preface 1

The Caterpillar 3

Chrysalis 143

Butterfly 207

Discussion Questions 229

About the Author 231

The Butterflies

When he steps into the room
and I look into his eyes
my stomach starts to turn
because he gives me butterflies
He's strong and secure
confident not conceited
He goes the extra mile
even when it's not needed
He has to have a life
and recognize when we need space
admitting when he's wrong
because I cannot be replaced
Last but not least
Providence will shape his life
and when he does find me
I'll be prepared to be his wife

Preface

Success was only a stone's throw away. She'd be like a caterpillar morphing into a butterfly. Patience would be her only virtue. But virtue was something she was struggling to have.

The Caterpillar

"Belle Isle is a 982-acre park that sits in the Detroit River between Michigan and Ontario, Canada. It's a Detroit gem that is rich with history and natural beauty."

Imani crept along the outskirts of the busy island, before easing her Jeep slightly to the right. She was never quite able to master the craft of parallel parking, so she surprised even herself when she managed to maneuver her vehicle almost perfectly between two cars.

Imani grabbed her bag, her blanket, and her sunglasses, before heading towards the water. She found herself struggling to smile as she strolled past the seemingly happy and carefree people. A young man and woman holding hands as they walked their dogs, a mother and father played Frisbee with their small children, and she was nearly run over by a gentleman as he sped past on rollerblades.

"Pardon me, little lady." The gentleman echoed as he carried on with his exercise.

Imani became annoyed. She was a diminutive woman, who was often mistaken for a young teenager and she hated it. She wanted to yell at the man and tell him that she was not a little lady but a twenty-three-year-old woman with the battle scars to prove it. But she relented, *for he meant no harm*. That gentleman was not the person responsible for her pain. Besides, she'd come to the park in search of peace.

Imani hurried toward the water where she found a nice quiet spot, away from all of the happiness. She had nothing against happiness, but it seemed as though happiness had something against her. *She could no longer seem to find it.* One day she could remember being happy, and the next day it just disappeared. Jumped ship. Took off and left, without ever saying goodbye. She'd found herself searching for it ever since.

Imani rolled out her blanket, sat with her legs crossed and took several deep breaths, as she tried to decompress. It was peaceful and serene. It gave her a chance to shut down and reboot. An opportunity to free her mind, and cleanse her soul, of all the toxic energies she'd recently allowed into her space.

She had a little over an hour before her shift would begin at Sanchez's lounge. She contemplated calling Mr. Sanchez and telling him that she didn't feel good. If he asked her what was wrong, she'd say, "she didn't feel like coming to work." Well, it wasn't necessarily a lie; she just had so much on her mind.

Imani reached inside her bag and pulled out the two envelopes. She sighed as she held her college class schedule in one hand, and a bill in the amount of six hundred dollars for the twin's daycare in the other. The words "Past Due" written across the top of the bill in big, bold, red, letters looked ominous; and it commanded her attention.

She needed to find a way to keep it together. If she could just hold on for another year, the sailing should be smoother. The goal was to be twenty-four and walking across the stage at University of Detroit Mercy with a degree in business. After that, she'd be able to go at it alone, if need be. She was confident that she could land a great job that paid enough money so that she could provide a stable home for her boys and herself.

But with the arduous task of juggling twins, school, a part-time job, and a man who suddenly lacked ambition and interest, her goals began to feel as if they were slowly slipping away. It was too difficult to maintain. She was becoming physically and mentally drained.

"Last of a dying breed" is what popped into Imani's head. She'd heard her father Peter McNair give that speech many times. He was a Marine Corps veteran, and what the world called a Baby Boomer. They were born following World War II when there was a temporary spike in births. That era ended in 1964.

Peter McNair said that during that era, many men wore suits and ties as part of their regular attire. They went to work and provided a stable home for their families. A woman was expected to follow one path: to marry young, start a family quickly, and devote her life to homemaking. Real men didn't want their wives to work. They prided themselves on being the sole providers, and the family structure seemed to be much stronger because of it.

He also said, "that once the feminist movement came about in the early '60s and '70s, things started to change. The women were tired of sitting at home. They felt trapped and unfulfilled. They wanted jobs and careers as well as equal rights and equal pay. They pretty much got what they wanted, but over fifty years later, single-parent homes have become socially acceptable, women are making just as much as the men, fast food is the new dinner menu, and the TV and video games are the ones rearing the children."

Peter McNair understood all too well why women wanted equal rights and equal pay; the men were no longer stepping up to the plate. But he was old school. His father was a strict, disciplinarian, from the South, who solely provided for his wife and eight children, so he made sure that he did the same with his wife and five children.

Although he was never able to afford designer labels, family vacations, or a large home, all their basic needs were met. The McNair family never went without and their home was filled with lots of love, nurturing, and firm discipline.

Peter and Brenda McNair had big dreams for all of their children. They wanted their children to reach heights that they never did because they became side-tracked by love — something neither of them regretted.

Their two teenaged sons were in high school, where they excelled in both sports and academics and their two oldest daughters went off to the armed services straight after high school. They claimed that they wanted to pay for school and see the world, but Imani knew that those were only half-truths. Her sisters tried to distance themselves from their strict, overbearing father, and that took courage. Something Imani didn't have. Even if she did have the courage to leave, where would she go?

Imani and her sisters were opposites. They were rebels, where Imani was modest and reserved. They broke all the house rules where she was diligent and more obedient.

She could recall on numerous occasions her sisters sneaking out of the house, sneaking boys into the house, stealing their father's car, and even skipping school. Many of those times they got busted, but the only problem was, her father could never figure out which sister was the actual culprit. Of course, he knew it wasn't Imani, because she was much younger and there was no way that she could pull off such an elaborate scheme as the older sisters. But since no one would tell, he would punish them all.

He never really believed in corporal punishment so when any of them stepped out of line, he'd make them wash the walls and windows, scrub the baseboards, clean out the garage, or sometimes he'd just put them under his "*house arrest*." His house arrest was the times that they'd just wished Peter McNair would whip out the old leather strap and get it over with.

After Imani graduated from high school, she opted to stay at home with her parents and attend "The University of Detroit Mercy." Although her father would never admit it, Imani was his favorite. She never gave him any real problems, unlike her sisters. He loved having her home. They developed a strong bond, and he managed to soften his approach and became more understanding. He didn't want to risk losing his youngest daughter because of his stern tough love methods.

Imani's relationship with her parents would soon be put to the test when she met and fell in love with Brandon Garrison her freshman year in college. This relationship would cause her father to have painful regrets as well as question his leniency towards his youngest daughter.

He would soon find that *"The one he suspected the least, was the one he should have watched the most."*

☙

Imani met Brandon Garrison the first week on campus. He noticed her first as he sat next to her in English class. Imani had always been quiet, shy, and focused. She took her studies seriously.

After the third day of class, Brandon sprinted up to Imani as she was heading to the school library.

"Excuse me." He said as he tried to catch his breath. "I sit a few seats over from you in English class. My name is Brandon Garrison, may I have your name?"

She gave a polite smile and said, "My name is Imani McNair, and it's very nice to meet you, Brandon."

He beamed, as he realized she was even prettier up close. "Well, that's such a pretty name for a pretty chocolate girl." He said with a grin.

She offered an awkward smile finding it strange that he'd open up the conversation with such an ambiguous statement. Heck! She knew that she was dark. She'd been dark all her life. She doesn't believe that there was a dark joke, chocolate joke or black girl joke, she hadn't heard. She wondered, what did he "really" mean by his statement? *That if she weren't dark, she wouldn't be pretty? Or she was only pretty in spite of being dark?*

Imani usually found those types of remarks offensive. Complimenting a person's beauty should never come with qualifiers or disclaimers. But the sincerity in his eyes told her she had to give him a free pass and the more she looked into his eyes, the more she noticed how beautiful they were.

She replied with, "And you have nice eyes for a tall guy." This statement made them both laugh.

"I get it now," Brandon said. "I'm sorry, but you are pretty."

As Imani continued to observe, she thought everything about him looked nice. He was tall, statuesque, with a gentle smile, low wavy hair, and perfectly straight teeth, held together by a retainer. He wore starched khaki pants, a white polo shirt, with polished black loafers. She was even more impressed by the fact that he wore a belt. Brandon looked like the kind of guy who was driven to school by a chauffeur. But most importantly, he looked like the type of guy she'd be proud to take home to her father.

Brandon gleamed as he spoke about himself. "I live at home with both of my parents. I am my mother's only child, but I have older twin brothers from my father. I graduated from an all-male prep school in Detroit. I don't have a girlfriend, and I can honestly say that it feels exhilarating to be in the presence of so many beautiful young ladies."

Imani smiled appreciating his honesty. "So, do you play any sports?" She asked.

Brandon answered with a chuckle. "Well, I played a little basketball in high school, but that's as far as my talents would take me. But I'm a beast, with a mean three-point shot, on NBA 2k." He laughed. "Bring on LeBron." He boasted. "When I'm not in class, you can find me at home in front of the television, playing NBA 2K, and eating Oreo cookies."

After he'd given her that brief synopsis of his life, she found him to be charming, with a great sense of humor.

Since Imani had never been a party girl, she found it appealing that Brandon was a guy of that same nature.

Imani shared her story with Brandon. She talked about her upbringing, her high school, and how she was majoring in business. She never did make it to the library that day, they sat on the bench and talked for close to two hours when a woman in a Ford Taurus stopped directly in front of the library and stared at them both.

Brandon hunched his shoulders and asked, “Is that for you?”

Imani hated to leave, but she knew if she didn’t move swiftly, her best friend LaShawn would honk the horn. LaShawn was a woman who was always on the move and she had very little patience.

Imani looked at Brandon apologetically and said, “That’s my ride, I have to go.”

As she rose from the bench, Brandon’s eyes softened, and he gently touched her hand. “Imani it was nice talking to you. I’d love to take you out sometime if that’s alright with you?”

Imani gave a flirtatious smile, and said, “I’d like that.”

The moment Imani stepped inside of LaShawn’s car the badgering would begin. “Who’s that nerdy looking guy?” LaShawn asked quizzically.

Imani chuckled at her question, guys like Brandon would never appeal to a girl like LaShawn. She only seemed to be attracted to the "renegades." "Bad boys had more fun," she claimed.

Imani responded, "His name is Brandon, and I happen to like nerds." She said while cutting her eyes at her friend.

"Well he looks like a square, but at least he's cute," LaShawn said teasingly.

Imani laughed and was unable to contain her excitement. "He asked me out, and I accepted."

LaShawn quickly pulled the car over to the side of the street and hit the brakes. "I can't believe it!" She said as she gave Imani a high five. "Well, it's about damn time, I thought you'd probably die a virgin."

Imani burst out laughing. "LaShawn, only you would say something crazy like that. It's not that serious. Now can you please take me to the salon so that you can do my hair?" Imani said as she removed her ponytail holder allowing her hair to rest freely upon her shoulders.

☙

LaShawn and Imani had been best friends since first grade. LaShawn lived a few blocks away from Imani in the home with her mother and grandmother. She and Imani rode the bus to school together every day. Imani remembered how adventurous those bus rides would be. LaShawn was the first to try everything. She started smoking early, wearing make-up early, driving early, and experimenting with boys early.

Imani's fondest memory was when they were starting sixth grade. LaShawn had gone and visited with an aunt in Virginia for the summer. When she returned, they both were as equally excited to see each other the first morning of school.

They'd arrived at the bus stop early. When Imani caught sight of her friend, she hardly recognized her. LaShawn looked like she was about sixteen instead of twelve. Her hair was no longer in cornrows, it hung loosely past her shoulders, and she wore a short skirt, a fitted t-shirt, a jean jacket, and a face full of make-up. Imani was speechless as she watched her friend confidently prance up to the bus stop, and strike a pose. LaShawn smiled and spread her arms and they embraced and laughed liked old friends do.

"Wow LaShawn, you look so grown-up." Said Imani fascinated by her boldness.

As the bus pulled up to the stop, LaShawn giggled as they stepped onto the bus. "Girl, I had an awesome summer in Virginia. My cousin's and I hung out at the mall, the beach, and the movies, all by ourselves, and I picked up some cool stuff," she said grabbing Imani's hand and ushering her to the back of the bus.

Once they were seated, LaShawn opened her purse so that Imani could peek inside. Imani's eyes protruded as she covered her mouth with both hands. She couldn't believe what she was seeing. That girl had lipstick, eyeshadow, mascara, cigarettes, and a lighter all stuffed inside of her purse.

"Imani, we're in middle school now, so we have to act like it." LaShawn said as she began to search around inside the purse. "Found them," she said with excitement in her voice. Imani's entire body stiffened, as LaShawn held up the bright pink lipstick and royal blue eyeshadow wearing a mischievous grin.

"Here put this on," LaShawn said assertively. Before Imani could object, LaShawn began to paint Imani's lips bright pink, before taking the eyeshadow and painting her eyelids royal blue. Imani knew her parents would kill her. She was only allowed to wear bubblegum flavored Chapstick, but she didn't dare say that to her friend. LaShawn paused for a few seconds as she surveyed her work. "Hmnnnnn, we need to highlight those cheeks." LaShawn fumbled around inside the purse again, until she found some blush. LaShawn took the blush brush and began to scrub Imani's cheeks with it. "This is not working," LaShawn said with a touch of frustration in her voice. "Your skin is too dark." LaShawn tossed the blush back inside of the purse and opted to use red lipstick. Imani sat there afraid to speak up as LaShawn smeared the thick creamy paste on each cheek. "That's much better," LaShawn said smiling, and seemingly impressed with her work. After a few minutes, she handed Imani a mirror. "What ya think?" She asked.

Imani looked at herself and hunched her shoulders. "I guess I like it."

Imani really didn't like it, but she didn't want to say that to LaShawn and risk being called a "*baby*." Imani thought that she looked silly, just like her friend.

LaShawn giggled and said, "You'll get used to it. Now let's get off this bus and go chase some boys."

Imani found that middle school was much different than elementary school. It was advanced and much faster. She and LaShawn didn't have any classes together, so that meant she had to walk around looking silly all alone. The stares, and people laughing made her feel uncomfortable. She couldn't wait to take that stuff off.

When the school day ended, and they were back on the bus, LaShawn appeared to be on a floating cloud. She opened her folder to show Imani the three love letters she'd received. LaShawn went on and on bragging about her day, and all the boys she'd met. That girl didn't shut up until the bus pulled up to their stop. Imani never said a word. In fact, she was happy that she didn't get the chance to speak because she had nothing exciting to report. She didn't get any love letters or phone numbers.

Once they exited the bus, and LaShawn was nowhere in sight, Imani grabbed some tissue from her bag and tried as best as she could to wipe the make-up off before she made it home. She scrubbed her cheeks until they started to burn.

When Imani made it to her block, she could see her mother wearing a big smile on her face as she stepped onto the porch. Her mother was excited to hear about her first day of middle school. "There's my big girl," she chanted.

As Imani ascended the steps, their eyes met. A look of scorn quickly replaced her mother's smile. "Imani!" She yelled. "Have you lost your darn mind? You look like a clown wearing that gaudy eye-makeup. Now go and wash it off right now!" Her mother demanded. Imani's heart nearly burst. She had forgotten all about the eyeshadow.

Mrs. McNair set Imani down on the living room sofa and said, "you are a child, and you are to stay in a child's place. You and that fast girl from around the corner are cut from two different cloths. You must remember to choose the company you keep wisely." Her mother went on and on, and when she got through with Imani that evening, Imani knew better than to ever pull that stunt again.

Imani felt so ashamed that she bowed her head. Mrs. McNair extended her index finger and lifted Imani's chin. *"The desire to stand out should be much greater than the desire to fit in." She* said as she offered her daughter a warm hug.

The next day, LaShawn approached the bus stop looking like nothing short of a "*streetwalker*," but this time she'd added a cigarette as an accessory. She offered it to Imani, and that's where Imani had to draw the line. No way, no how, was she going to get caught up in that.

LaShawn laughed and shook her head in pity. "Imani we can't stay babies forever ya know." Imani refused to budge. "Oh well, suit yourself. More boys for me." LaShawn said as she continued to laugh.

Throughout their school years, LaShawn never asked her friend to smoke or wear make-up again. LaShawn understood that Imani had strict parents, where she did not. Imani was relieved that she was no longer under pressure and yet they were still able to remain friends. Imani loved hearing all the exciting stories and rendezvous that LaShawn shared with her. Imani would hate to give that up as she would secretly start to live her life vicariously through her friend.

Once Imani met Brandon Garrison, she leaned on her friend more than she ever had before. Imani considered LaShawn to be an "expert" when it came to dating. She was experienced, and Imani believed that LaShawn had all the answers.

☙

The next day Brandon met Imani in front of the library. They sat and talked a little more when he said, "tell your ride there's no need to pick you up tomorrow, I want to take you out."

Imani smiled, and accepted, although she was a bit nervous having never been on a real date before. Imani had gone to the prom with her childhood friend Kevin Black, but she didn't consider that to be an actual date since their families were close friends. But since Kevin was homeschooled and she didn't have a date, his family and her parents thought it would be a great idea if he escorted her to the prom. Kevin was what people commonly referred to as a nerd. He had all the traits — the glasses, flood pants, and the weird haircut. Imani wasn't physically attracted to him, but she cared about him as a friend so she didn't make a fuss. She and Kevin went to the prom, ate from the buffet, sat at the table and watched others dance, and they posed for a photo. They did all of this merely to satisfy both families.

Imani wasn't too concerned about her date with Brandon. She had a pretty good idea of what to expect since she'd heard plenty of good and bad stories about the do's and don'ts of dating.

LaShawn's number one rule was "Don't kiss on the first date." When Imani asked her why, LaShawn said, "Because that means he's your boyfriend." Imani thought that sounded silly and didn't make sense, but hey what did she know? Her friend was the expert, so Imani decided that she wouldn't kiss Brandon on the first date.

☙

Brandon pulled in front of the library in a late model black Dodge Charger. Imani was surprised that a first-year student in college would have such a nice car. She also reveled in his chivalry, as he opened and closed the car door for her.

Brandon noticed Imani's new look right away. She had traded the jeans and a college t-shirt for a pretty, navy-blue dress with a fitted sweater. Her hair was different also. He wanted to ask if she'd changed her look just for him, but he wasn't sure if that was an appropriate question to ask, so he decided to play it safe. "You look lovely as always."

Imani gave a pleasant smile. "Thank you."

"Do you like pizza?" He asked.

"Who doesn't like pizza?" She responded.

"Well, what would you like on your pizza?" Brandon asked with a soft smile.

"Just vegetables," Imani said returning the same smile.

Brandon retrieved his cell phone and dialed a number. "Hello Maria, I'm bringing company home, and we'd like to have two personal pizzas. One with vegetables and the other with meat." He paused for a few seconds before thanking Maria and hanging up the phone.

Imani was aghast. "You call your mother, Maria?"

Brandon laughed. "No. She's our housekeeper."

"Oh wow!" I've never met anyone with a housekeeper before." She said surprisingly.

"She doesn't live with us or anything. She only comes in a few times a week. My parents have been on vacation so she's there getting things prepared for their return." He said like it was no big deal.

Imani responded with a casual, "Oh!"

Brandon's home was huge. It was tucked away in an upscale subdivision in Detroit. Their house along with the others looked like something out of "The Fresh Prince of Bel Air." Imani couldn't contain herself as he pulled into the back of the house into his own designated parking spot.

"What did you say your parents did for a living?" She asked.

Brandon responded, "My mother is a retired fashion model, and my father is an engineer who owns a software company. I plan to follow in my father's footsteps so that one day I can help run the business alongside my brothers."

"Wow!" Said Imani. "Well, my mom is a housewife, who volunteers at the schools and my father is a postal worker by day, and he does light mechanic work in our garage in the evenings." Imani wasn't ashamed at what her parents did for a living; she just hoped Brandon wouldn't think less of her because of it.

Brandon gave a reassuring smile. "That's cool."

She was pleased with his casual response. It temporarily put her mind at ease. "Brandon, you are a very fortunate young man."

Brandon beamed, "Yes I am. I'm fortunate enough to be in the presence of a pretty girl like you." He moved in closer until their noses began to touch. Imani started to have that funny feeling inside her stomach, as they shared their very first kiss.

Oh well! She thought, LaShawn's number one rule just went out the window.

The inside of the home was just as spectacular as the outside. It had cathedral ceilings, elegant crystal chandeliers, beautiful wood cabinetry, shiny floors, fresh floral arrangements throughout the house, and so much more. Imani was overwhelmed, as it seemed like you could put her parent's entire home, inside of their kitchen.

Brandon escorted her to the powder room that sat right off from the kitchen. Imani looked around at the beautifully decorated room thinking that it was one of the prettiest powder rooms she'd ever seen.

After they ate their pizzas, he gave her a grand tour. Imani tipped toed through the home in awe. Everything had its place, including the oil painting of an elegant woman dressed in all black, wearing a string of pearls, with perfect posture that hung over the fireplace in the formal dining room.

"Who's that beautiful lady?" asked Imani.

"That's my mother. My father had that painting commissioned for her birthday."

Imani then spotted a collection of ornately framed portraits on a small table. One of the pictures was dated back to the late 1800s, and all the men looked very prestigious.

Brandon pointed to the portraits. "It's four generations of Garrison men in these pictures. I make number five." He said with honor.

Imani thought it was fascinating how the Garrison's wealthy pedigree could be traced back to the late 1800s. It caused her to wonder about her family's history.

Brandon gently grabbed Imani by the hand and said, "Let me take you to my favorite spot in the house."

He led Imani into a large room, which looked like an arcade or even a movie theater. Framed posters of Isaiah Thomas, Chauncy Billups, Michael Jordan, LeBron James, Magic Johnson and other NBA players whom she did not recognize hung on the walls. The room was equipped with a flat screen television, a surround sound audio system, movie theater seats, and a popcorn machine, as well as Brandon's PlayStation and X Box games.

Imani stepped into the center of the room, raised her arms and did a 360 spin. "Brandon this is so freaking cool. My brothers would love this."

Brandon quickly stepped over to the sound system. "What type of music would you like to hear?"

"I love Motown," Imani said.

Brandon picked up the remote, clicked a few buttons and the strains of Marvin Gaye crooned through the speakers. Imani smiled as she hummed along to the beat.

Once he had her all settled in, he handed her the remote, gave her a quick tutorial and dashed for his video game.

"Do you mind if I play my game now?" He eagerly asked as he picked up his headphones.

"Not at all" she laughed. "I have more than enough music to keep me occupied."

Brandon rushed to give Imani a quick peck on the cheek before flopping down on the sofa.

Imani initially found Brandon's love of the video game amusing. But as time went by, she realized just how much that game meant to him. He went through a plethora of emotions. He clapped, threw his hands up, cursed the refs, cried foul, and huffed out loud. She couldn't believe how worked up he'd become while playing that game.

Suddenly a tall, slender, older woman peeked inside the room and softly said, "Hellooo." Imani recognized the beautiful woman from the oil painting. She smiled and returned the hello.

Brandon was so engrossed in his game that he never noticed her standing there. Imani tapped him on the shoulder. Brandon looked away for a second. "Hey, Mom." He said before turning his attention back on his game. Imani's eyes became wide. Brandon suddenly jumped up from his game after he'd realized what he had done. "Oh, Mom hey. Welcome home." Brandon pointed over at Imani. "This is my girlfriend, Imani."

Mrs. Garrison and Imani both looked surprised. His mother could never recall her son refer to anyone as his girlfriend and Imani had never been labeled as a girlfriend before, but Imani liked how it sounded. *Wow! LaShawn really knew her stuff.* A kiss can really lead to a relationship. Imani whispered to herself.

His mother walked over and greeted Imani with a hug. "I'm Mrs. Garrison, pleased to meet you, my dear. I don't believe I've ever met any girl Brandon has dated. You must be special."

Imani smiled. "It's a pleasure to meet you as well."

His mother asked, "Brandon have you two eaten? If not, I can have Maria fix you both something before she leaves."

"We're fine. We had pizza a few hours ago." Brandon replied.

"Well I'm going to retire for the evening, I'll have her fix you something for later." His mother said before offering one last smile as she exited the room.

Imani thought his mother was lovely, but from the sound of things, she wasn't done nurturing. Brandon seemed to be spoiled.

Before the evening ended, Brandon was ready to introduce Imani to his father. She was nervous, as she was afraid of saying the wrong thing. Brandon could see it in her eyes.

"Imani, my father, is one of the nicest men you'll ever want to meet. There's no need to be nervous. Just relax and be yourself."

Just as Brandon had said, Mr. Garrison was a pleasant, mild-mannered, friendly man who looked like an older, balding version of his son. He sat in an oversized leather chair in his study, wearing a thick housecoat, smoking a cigar, and reading a golfing magazine. The introduction went smooth. He asked very few questions. He just smiled, shook Imani's hand, and told them both to be careful out on the road.

When they made it back to Brandon's car, Imani said, "Your father is simply adorable."

Brandon looked over at Imani and proudly said, "I think he's the greatest."

Imani looked over as Brandon settled into the car and gently held his hand. "My father is much different from your father. In fact, he is the antithesis of your dad. So Brandon, buckle up because you're in for one hell of a ride."

☙

Mr. McNair stepped from the garage wearing a baseball cap, soiled coveralls, oily work boots, and carrying a wrench in his hand. Imani had just called out to him.

He hugged Imani and said, "Hello baby girl. So how was school today?"

"It was great." Imani said as she cleared her throat. "Ummm Dad, I want you to meet Brandon. Brandon, this is my Dad, Mr. McNair." She said nervously.

The bald but compact, muscular, older man gave Brandon a good once-over before he spoke. Peter McNair could detect right away, that Brandon wasn't your typical, black, urban male. Brandon looked to be well polished, and judging by the car he drove; he could also tell that he was privileged.

Mr. McNair extended his oily right hand as Brandon reluctantly clasped hands with the older man. Mr. McNair gave a tight squeeze being sure to transfer as much of the oil and grease as possible to Brandon's now wilting hand. Brandon attempted to pull away but was met with great resistance as Mr. McNair continued to shake his hand.

Mr. McNair let out a loud, hearty laugh. "What's a wrong son, you're afraid of getting your hands dirty?"

Brandon looked a bit uncomfortable, but he managed to conjure up a smile." He responded with, "No sir."

Mr. McNair gave Brandon a hard pat on the back and said, "Good. Now let's go inside the house so that we can eat."

Imani was upset at her father, but she didn't let on to Brandon. She knew what he meant by offering Brandon his dirty hand. He gave every male that tried to date any one of his daughters a standard "Litmus test." If it was something as simple as blowing the horn in front of their home, bringing them home after curfew, or making one of his daughters cry, he used that as a way of testing their manliness. He believed that all men should be strong. Her father felt great disdain toward weak men. Her sisters hated when their father did that. It always chased their boyfriends away. Imani would sit back and laugh when this happened. But now that it was happening to her, she didn't find any humor in it at all.

They all entered through the back door. Mr. McNair immediately excused himself and headed to the basement so that he could change out of his work clothes.

Imani removed her shoes, and Brandon followed suit. Mrs. McNair stood up from the table as Imani introduced Brandon. Mrs. McNair gave a warm and welcoming smile. "It's so nice to meet you, young man."

Brandon responded with, "It's a pleasure to meet you as well."

Mrs. McNair asked, "Well if you two are hungry, there's fresh chicken that I just took out of the oven. Brandon, you are more than welcome to stay for dinner."

Brandon looked at Mrs. McNair with a smile and said, "Thank you. I'd love to stay for dinner."

"Imani, show Brandon where the bathroom is so you guys can wash your hands while I fix everyone's plate," Mrs. McNair said.

Imani pointed Brandon in the direction of the bathroom. She began to feel a bit nervous as he walked away. She thought of his beautiful, spacious home and wondered what went through his mind when he came to hers. Her house had no cathedral ceilings, fancy chandeliers, long hallways or winding staircases; their bathroom was just outside the kitchen, to the left. But her mother kept their home neat, clean, and nicely decorated. They had a comfortable reclining sofa in the living room, a wooden coffee table with an artificial flower arrangement on top, and an entertainment center with a flat screen television.

After they'd finished their meal, Brandon looked over at Mrs. McNair and said, "That tasted delicious, and you have a lovely home. Thanks again for having me."

Mrs. McNair wore a proud smile. "It's our pleasure."

Mr. McNair then said, "So Brandon, tell us a little something about yourself."

Brandon gave Mr. McNair the introduction that he'd given Imani about being an only child with two older half-brothers. He spoke about graduating from an all-male prep high school, and how his basketball career started and ended there. Brandon also mentioned how he planned to become an engineer.

"That's very impressive." Mr. McNair said. "Do you mind if I ask what your parents do for a living?"

Imani began to grow nervous. She didn't know how her father would react, or what he'd say, once he found out that Brandon had wealthy parents.

"My father works in computer software, and my mother is retired from the fashion industry," Brandon said casually.

Mr. and Mrs. McNair gave an approving smile as they both slowly nodded their heads up and down.

Mr. McNair added, “With parents like that, you must live in one of those upscale towns like Bloomfield Hills or Birmingham somewhere?”

After Mr. McNair said this, Imani knew where this was leading, but Brandon was smart. He didn’t take the bait. “No sir, I was raised right here in Detroit, and so were my parents.”

Imani let out a shallow breath as she smiled on the inside. Brandon was doing great, and she appreciated how he complimented their home and downplayed his family’s wealth. “*Halfway there, Brandon.”* She whispered to herself.

The very next moment, Mr. McNair cleared his throat, straightened his posture, and his facial expression turned serious.

“Oh boy, he’s about to get started,” Imani said to herself. Peter McNair was starting to revert to his old ways. The subject would soon turn from general questions, and it would ultimately lead to politics. He often claimed that he could gauge a person by their political views.

Imani looked over at her mother with pleading eyes. Mrs. McNair gave Imani a slight nod, as she also knew what was about to happen next.

Mr. McNair spoke. His tone was no longer soft, but serious and direct. "So, Brandon, what makes you interested in our daughter?"

Brandon seemed nervous, but he managed to keep it together. "Well because she's nice, and she's smart, and she's beautiful."

Mr. McNair smiled before he cleared his throat again. "So, do you plan to date my daughter exclusively?" Brandon straightened his posture and swallowed the lump in his throat before he offered a response.

Imani felt like melting, as she knew that the questions would only get tougher. She wished that she could stand up to her father.

Brenda McNair noticed the sadness in Imani's eyes and quickly intervened. "Pete, stop it! Leave these kids alone! They've just met." She said assertively.

Imani paused before letting out a heavy sigh. She looked over at her mother and gave a modest smile, as she was the only person in their household that could control Peter McNair. Although Brenda McNair would never undermine his authority, she knew how to rein him in if she believed he was going too far.

Mr. McNair immediately softened up. "Ok, Brenda. I'm just trying to see where this young man's head is at." Mrs. McNair gave him that look where her eyes became small, her lips tightly pursed, and her head tilted. *It worked every time.* Imani didn't know what type of special powers her mother had, but she was sure glad she had them.

Mrs. McNair suddenly rose from the table and said, "Would you guys like some iced tea?" Everyone said yes, and things managed to run smoothly from that point on. Mr. McNair and Brandon talked about sports for the rest of the evening. *You couldn't go wrong with that.*

As the evening came to a close, Mr. McNair stared directly into Brandon's eyes as he shook his hand, "Son, just continue to make my daughter smile and we won't have any problems."

Brandon responded with a smile. "Mr. McNair, I promise that I'll take good care of her."

Imani was relieved when her father glanced over at her and winked his eye.

She and Brandon stood outside of his car and locked into an embrace. Imani stared intensely into his eyes and said, "You told your mother that I was your girlfriend, but I don't ever recall you asking me that question."

Brandon gave that infectious smile. "Imani McNair, will you be my girlfriend?"

She kissed him softly on his lips. "Yes, Brandon I will be your girlfriend."

Imani found Brandon amazing. *"They were simply two young people, from two completely different worlds, yet they somehow managed to find themselves attracted to one another."*

ଔ

Imani and Brandon had been seeing each other for a few weeks when Mrs. McNair noticed a drastic change in Imani's behavior. Imani smiled all the time. *Even when there was nothing to really smile about.*

"You really like this Brandon huh?" Mrs. McNair asked.

"Yes, Mom I do," Imani said with a bashful smile.

"Well do you think it's time for me to take you to the doctor so that we can get you on some form of birth control? Your father and I want you to finish school before you even think about getting married and starting a family."

Imani could see the disappointed look in her mother's eyes when she said, "Yes."

She knew that her mother was hoping that she had said, "No" but Imani couldn't bring herself to do that. Imani meeting and falling for Brandon surprised even herself. She was the only child of her parents that they believed would save herself for marriage. Imani chuckled as she once thought that herself.

When Imani was in high school, she thought that most boys her age were silly and immature. She'd see the guys that LaShawn would date and thumb her nose at them. They were the outcasts. They sagged their pants, smoked weed and cigarettes, and skipped class. Many girls seemed to be attracted to those types of boys but not Imani.

There were a few nice guys, but Imani didn't seem to find anything interesting about them either. They were smart, or maybe even cute, but many of them were often too shy, too serious, or they seemed to lack the confidence to ask a girl out.

The only real crush Imani ever had was in high school. He was her substitute gym teacher, Mr. Lawrence. He was at least ten years older than her, but she secretly liked his style. He was intelligent, dressed neat, and very handsome. She never told anyone about the crush, not even LaShawn because she knew she'd get teased. So instead of going out on dates with silly boys, Imani liked to hang out with her father on the weekends. They'd sit in his basement, and he'd spin the records. They would listen to Aretha Franklin, Smokey Robinson, The Supremes, Anita Baker, and so many others. Her mother would supply the snacks and she, and her daddy would have their very own party in the basement.

Imani falling hard for Brandon seemed surreal. It was as if he was created especially for her. He wasn't a bad boy, but a nice guy who wasn't afraid of going after what he wanted. He had just the perfect amount of balance, so she didn't want to offer her mother any false hope. She loved Brandon.

The next day Mrs. McNair took Imani to the doctor where he prescribed for Imani birth control pills. "Imani this is not an endorsement but a precaution." Mrs. McNair repeated what the doctor had said. "Remember that the pill won't prevent sexually transmitted diseases, and you must use condoms for the first seven days before the pill would become fully effective." Mrs. McNair said firmly with a hint of sadness in her voice.

Imani had heard what her mother had said about using extra protection, but it was as if she'd never said it.

ଓ

Imani had been at the salon with LaShawn all day. She was her last customer.

"Imani, after I finish your hair, I have something special to show you." Lashawn said with a massive grin on her face.

Imani was excited, "What is it?" She asked.

LaShawn said, "You'll just have to wait and see."

It was a little after six o'clock in the evening when they'd left the shop. They stopped by "The Pizza Palace" and ordered Imani's favorite vegetarian pizza before they headed to their destination.

She noticed that LaShawn was driving in the opposite direction of their homes. "Where are we headed?" Imani asked.

LaShawn continued to smile, “It’s a surprise.”

They soon passed a CVS pharmacy, a liquor store, a beauty supply, and a check-cashing place before they turned right, onto an unfamiliar street. They drove another two blocks before they pulled into an apartment complex that was located on the west side of Detroit, not too far from their homes.

Imani was a little uncomfortable, as she had no idea where they were headed. It wasn’t the most fabulous apartment complex, but it wasn’t the worst. There also weren’t very many buildings in the complex.

“LaShawn who lives here?” Imani asked nervously.

LaShawn grabbed the pizza box and looked over at Imani and said, “Oh calm down, it’s safe here. Just follow me.”

As Imani followed LaShawn up to the building, there were a few middle-aged black guys sitting at a picnic table playing dominos. “Hey, LaShawn.” The guys all said wearing big smiles across their faces. LaShawn smiled and waved at them all. A few ladies who were headed out the building spoke to her as well. It was evident that everyone knew and liked her.

LaShawn pulled out a key, and she and Imani hiked up a flight of stairs landing on the third floor. LaShawn opened the door to a nice, neat, and clean two-bedroom apartment that had minimal furniture. There was a sofa, a table, and a few barstools that sat under the counter in the kitchen.

Imani looked surprised. “So whose place is this?”

LaShawn did her famous “boss lady” pose and said, “It’s mine.”

Imani couldn’t believe it. The girl was only nineteen, and she had her own apartment. Imani was proud of her. LaShawn was one of the hardest working girls Imani had ever met. So, if anyone deserved it, she sure did.

LaShawn was starting to make a great life for herself, considering that she’d skipped college. She claimed that she wasn’t academically inclined, but where she lacked in academics, she made up for it with her creativity. Anything LaShawn set her mind to, she could do it. The girl had a vision early on.

Imani recalled how she opted out all the tough classes in high school like chemistry, calculus, and geometry, opting to take art, cosmetology, and home economics. LaShawn would soon become the neighborhood beautician. She braided, pressed, or put hair extensions, in just about every girl’s hair in the neighborhood. She knew how to do makeovers, nails, and even design clothes. Everyone paid her well.

In high school, LaShawn never charged Imani. When LaShawn needed to practice a new hairstyle or wanted someone to rock some gear she’d made, Imani was that person.

Imani stood in LaShawn’s apartment proud that she was able to witness “the fruits of her labor” finally paying off. "Wow LaShawn, you really are something," Imani said wearing a wide, proud smile.

LaShawn returned the smile. "Thank you. It's not much, and it's not very fancy, but I can take my time and make it my own. I've been saving up money since high school. I knew that once I graduated, I'd move out. My mother and grandmother have been running a shop at that flea market since I was a young girl. I love those two, but it seems like the more they sell, the more they collect. Our home was just cluttered with stuff. We've lived like that our entire lives and I didn't want to continue to live that way, so I had to move on. My cousin is the manager of this building, so she helped me with the process." Lashawn said proudly.

Imani was still in awe. "You're awesome!"

LaShawn grabbed some paper plates from the cabinets along with two wine glasses. She opened the refrigerator and grabbed a bottle of wine. Imani's eyes widened, as she took a deep breath. LaShawn laughed. "Don't worry I know you can't go home smelling like alcohol, so I have some apple juice especially for you." Imani exhaled as she laughed along with her friend. She knew better than to ask LaShawn about where she got the wine from. *LaShawn had been grown her entire life, and it seemed as if she could make anything happen.*

LaShawn poured herself a glass of wine, and she poured Imani a glass of juice. They clinked glasses and said, "Cheers."

LaShawn put a slice of pizza on each of their plates. As LaShawn bit down on her pizza, she noticed that Imani wore a big frown across her face. "What's wrong? This is your favorite pizza."

Imani said, "It doesn't smell…." Then she suddenly darted off to the bathroom.

LaShawn dropped her plate and ran behind her friend. She stopped just outside the door and was startled as she witnessed Imani's head practically inside the toilet. Imani coughed and coughed until everything she had eaten that day was inside the bowl.

LaShawn stared at her friend in horror. "Imani, what's wrong?"

Imani looked at her and said, "I don't know, I guess that pizza didn't sit too well in my stomach."

LaShawn asked, "When was the last time you had your period?"

Imani looked confused, "Ummmm it's been a little over a month. Why do you ask?"

"Well because I think you may be pregnant," LaShawn said, cautiously.

Imani looked frightened. "No, I can't be pregnant, I'm on birth control pills."

LaShawn responded, "I remember when you told me that your mom took you to the clinic and you were put on the pill, and also remember you saying that you and Brandon had a romantic evening the very next day. Did you remember that you were supposed to use protection for the first seven days before the pill would work?"

Imani said, "Oh my God. I didn't even think about that. I totally blocked that out."

LaShawn didn't want to alarm Imani, so she said, "you're probably fine; maybe it really was the pizza." LaShawn reached inside the closet and handed Imani a clean face towel, toothbrush, and washcloth. "Clean yourself up. I'll be right back."

Within twenty minutes LaShawn was back inside of the apartment. She had a small plastic bag in her hand. She pulled out a pregnancy test kit and said, "Here you go."

It didn't take long before Imani stepped from the bathroom holding the stick in her hand with tears in her eyes. She was pregnant.

LaShawn stepped over to her friend and gave her a big embrace "I'm here for you no matter what."

ଓ

The ride to the Garrison's with her parents was a quiet and somber one. Imani was now eight weeks pregnant, and she was carrying twins.

Mr. McNair was disappointed. He hadn't said much to Imani since she and Brandon shared their news. He avoided her at all cost by working overtime at the post office, staying at the gym with her brothers, or he worked out in his garage. But now that she and Brandon had decided that they wanted to get married and move out on their own, he was forced out of hiding.

Mrs. McNair, on the other hand, was disheartened, but there wasn't much she could say. She tried to reason with her husband, reminding him that they too were young newlyweds, but it fell on deaf ears. Peter McNair claimed that times were different back then. Imani didn't see much difference. She believed that times were better and that she and Brandon would have it easier.

The minute Peter McNair turned onto the Garrison's block Imani could sense the discomfort of both of her parents. Her father slowed the car, as they both seemed to stare in awe. Her parents believed they understood what was behind Imani's motivation to start a family and move out. The Garrison's could offer her things they could not.

Maria, the Garrison's housekeeper, answered the door wearing a graceful smile. "Hello Imani, it's great to see you again." She said. Imani returned the gesture and introduced her parents. The Garrison's stood directly behind Maria, and there was one big introduction.

"You have a beautiful home." Mrs. McNair said to Mrs. Garrison.

"Thank you," replied Mrs. Garrison with a soft smile.

Peter McNair just offered a half smile. He'd come here to discuss their children, and he wasn't in the mood for all the extras. But he managed to ease up a bit once Mr. Garrison extended his hand and introduced himself. "My name is Allen Garrison, but you may call me Allen." Brandon's father said in a friendly manner.

"I'm Peter McNair, but you can call me Pete." Imani's father said with a slight smile as they shook hands.

Brandon and Imani sat there like two small children as Mr. Garrison spoke. He spoke of how they were wonderful children, and how he believed it was essential that they both finished school before they got married and moved out on their own.

Mr. Garrison talked about how he had married and had a set of twin boys himself by his high school sweetheart when he was nineteen. He talked about how he had always been a very ambitious man, and instead of going to college right away, he used most of his inheritance from his late grandfather, to start a construction business. Mr. Garrison put in long hours and was making a good living for his family, but that marriage failed three years later because he was never home. His first wife couldn't handle the long hours, and being home alone with their kids, so she filed for divorce. Mr. Garrison said that for years his younger children suffered greatly because he and his ex-wife were not mature enough to handle marriage or divorce. His divorce caused him to go into a deep depression. He lost everything because of it, and it took him ten years to rebuild and land back on his feet.

Mr. Garrison looked over at Brandon and Imani and spoke with sincerity. "You kids are still young." He stepped over to his son so that he could look him in the eyes. Mr. Garrison raised his right hand and rested it on Brandon's shoulder. He let out a heavy sigh, "Brandon, you have so much growing to do. You remind me of myself when I was your age, and I cannot, with good conscience, allow you to repeat the same mistakes that I made." Brandon listened intently. He didn't utter a word.

Mr. Garrison removed his hand from Brandon's shoulder and stepped over to his wife. She stood and held her husband's hand as he continued to speak. "Linda and I would like to propose an agreement. If you two agree to hold off on marriage and wait until you both finish college, we will pay for your wedding and buy you a house of your own. In the meantime, we have plenty of room here. We will have the entire basement remodeled for you two, and since it has a separate entrance, you will have all the privacy that you need."

When Mr. Garrison finished speaking, Peter McNair spoke up. "Allen, my wife and I couldn't agree with you more about these two being too young and immature for marriage. But I cannot condone my child living under a roof with a man who is not her husband. We didn't raise Imani that way, and I'm really uncomfortable with this arrangement. We have a home, and we will make room for our child and those unborn babies."

Mr. Garrison apologized to the McNair's. "I'm sorry if I offended you, but I really didn't know what else to do. These two were going to run off and get married without telling us. If Brandon hadn't asked his mother for his birth certificate, we wouldn't have known. I don't want them to end up on the streets struggling because we are too stubborn to accept reality."

Peter and Brenda McNair eyed Imani in total shock. Imani lowered her head. They were blindsided. They had no idea that Imani and Brandon were planning to run off and get married without telling anyone.

Peter McNair looked over at his wife and said, "I've heard enough. I've already expressed my displeasure, and I stand firm on my beliefs." He looked at Allen Garrison and thanked him for everything, although he wasn't quite sure what he was actually thanking him for.

Peter McNair was not a college-educated man, but he was no fool. He could see right through Allen Garrison. He was protecting his son's interest. They were rich, filthy rich, and it sure as heck didn't come from winning the lottery. That man was born wealthy, and if his son married Imani, Allen Garrison knew she'd be entitled to most of his son's inheritance if it failed. Peter McNair knew that his daughter was too young, and too naïve, to understand that.

He looked over at Imani and pleaded one last time.

"Imani, moving in here with Brandon is not the answer. Moving out and starting a family is a serious commitment, and I cannot give you my blessings at this time. You both are so young. Throughout the years, things will change, people will change, and sometimes it won't be for the better. I believe you both should rethink this. Imani, we will make room for you and the twins at our home. Brandon can come and see the children whenever he likes. If the love is real, it will withstand. You are both great kids; however, you two have a lot of growing to do."

Imani looked as though she were going to cry. Peter McNair felt terrible for his daughter, but he had to stand firm on his beliefs. He looked at her once more and said, "Imani are you coming home with us or are you staying here?"

Imani looked sadly at her father and said, "I'm staying."

Peter McNair looked sternly at his wife and said, "Well it's settled. Brenda let's go."

That day in the Garrison's home Imani officially broke her parents' hearts. No, they didn't disown her; however, the relationship with her dad was never quite the same.

Her agreeing to stay with the Garrison's made her father feel as though she favored them over him. That wasn't the case. She loved Brandon, and she just wanted to be with him.

ᘓ

As Imani sat by the water and thought about she and Brandon's relationship throughout the years, she regretted compromising. She wished they had eloped. It seemed as though it would have been easier. They have children, and they should have been married. She believes that if his parents stopped nurturing him and being his safety net, Brandon would stand on his own. He would try harder to make their relationship work. Now five years later, she realized her father was right. People do change, and it's not always for the better.

Imani knew that she couldn't take off work. Sanchez's Lounge and its lively atmosphere was an outlet. It temporarily took her mind off her troubles with Brandon, and it gave her an escape from her reality.

She took an exasperated breath, neatly folded the daycare bill, her class schedule, and placed them back inside of her bag. She hopped in her Jeep and headed toward Sanchez's lounge.

ᘓ

Mr. Sanchez and his brother Hector greeted her at the door. Imani smiled as she stepped behind the bar to start her shift. As Imani placed her bag under the counter, her cell phone chimed informing her that there was a video message. She let out a heavy sigh and rolled her eyes so far up her head until only the whites were showing.

She relaxed and hit the video of LaShawn and the two beautiful young waitresses, who also worked at the lounge. They had the non-guilty pleasure of taking a weekend vacation to Las Vegas courtesy of the boss Mr. Sanchez. He'd offered to pay Imani's way as well, but that wasn't who she was. Although tempted, she couldn't do it. She was a committed, responsible, and dedicated parent, unlike Brandon, who was a spoiled "man-child."

"Heeeeeey Imani girl." LaShawn and the two inebriated young ladies sang, giggled and waved into the camera. They all were wearing skimpy bikini's, with long "Indian Remy" wavy hair, down to the center of their backs. They each were holding a bottle of champagne, soaking in a hot tub.

"Did you like the gift I left for you?" LaShawn asked as she continued to smile. "I almost had you." She teased. "One day I will be successful at getting you to let all that beautiful hair down and drag you on the plane with us. Those boys will be fine with their daddy. At least you know they'll be safe since he doesn't leave the house and is married to that video game."

LaShawn curled her lips expressing her irritation. “Oh well, at least you're still working, I thought you would have quit by now. Baby steps I guess.”

LaShawn giggled as they all raised their glasses and blew kisses into the camera ending the video.

Imani half smiled and let out a saddened chuckle responding with lots of smiling emoji's. They looked like they were having a blast.

LaShawn was right about one thing; she did almost have her on that plane. A small fraction of Imani was so close to saying “*screw it*” and walking away from adulthood for just one weekend. She imagined how good it would feel to drop everything and run away from Brandon, the children, and all her other responsibilities. Something she'd never done before.

LaShawn was the one who gave her the speech about getting out there and showing Brandon she could make it on her own. “Girl put those babies in daycare, get you a job, and show him you don't need him or his parents. I bet he will get it together then. You're a good woman; better than any young woman I've ever known because I ain't giving up my young life to be a *play housewife* for anybody.” LaShawn chastened.

LaShawn then introduced Imani to her boss Carlos Sanchez. He owned the bar and grill in downtown Detroit for over twenty years. His younger brother Hector managed it.

Mr. Sanchez was a kind, wealthy and generous, Hispanic man in his fifty's. He had lots of connections. He received free tickets and invitations to all sorts of events. Since he'd recently lost his lovely wife of thirty years to a lengthy illness, he claimed that going to those events no longer excited him. So, he gave the tickets away. He said the only reason he hadn't retired from his business was that it kept him going. Being around happy crowds of people eased the pain of losing his wife. It brought him joy, so he didn't mind sharing his wealth.

Mr. Sanchez understood that if he took care of his employees, they would take care of him. That's why every week or so, he seemed to send at least a couple of girls on vacation, to a concert, a play or even a ball game.

Mr. Sanchez offered Imani tickets on several occasions, but she never accepted. He somewhat admired and pitied her modesty at the same time. He'd overhear LaShawn giving her pep talks about her relationship with her boyfriend often. He knew of Imani's struggles with being a young woman, trying to uplift a man, raise children, work, and go to school. He always put extra money in her pay because he knew she wouldn't take a handout, although she seemed as though she could desperately use one.

Imani had to admit, LaShawn throwing Brandon's behavior in her face in front of the other ladies hurt like hell. She guessed she'd asked for it by often complaining to her about her relationship with Brandon and his love of video games.

Imani was also beginning to doubt what LaShawn had said about Brandon stepping up once he found out she was working. She thought back to the heated exchange she'd had with Brandon earlier. Their relationship was on the brink. Imani realized that instead of stepping up, he was stepping further away.

☙

In the beginning, Imani was happy. The arrangement with his parents was working out fine. They had a comfortable life, they didn't have to worry about bills, and the kids had everything that they needed. But as time went on, Imani noticed how comfortable Brandon had become. As long as he had his gaming systems, junk food, and a cold beer, there were no complaints from him whatsoever. He'd graduated from school five months earlier, and Imani still had not. She took the first year off to bond with the twins and now she was only going to school part-time.

Brandon never did go to work for his father as he'd promised; he decided to take a management position at Game Stop. He said that going to work for his dad, really didn't interest him anymore. He loved working at the video game store. Brandon was slowly changing the rules, and Imani didn't like what she was seeing. She feared there wouldn't be a marriage, and she'd be stuck in his parent's basement permanently.

The tipping point for her was when she came home from school and noticed he'd bought the three-year-old twins a gaming system of their own. Seeing her babies so engrossed in a video game on the big screen television was so appalling to her. When she cut the video game off, they threw a tantrum. Imani did not want her sons to be addicted to a video game, like their father. Brandon claimed it kept them occupied but Imani knew better. Brandon bought the video game as a proxy. Instead of Brandon having to interact with the boys physically, he'd let the video game do it.

Imani knew at that moment that she needed to start working on an exit strategy. That's when she decided to take LaShawn's advice and put the kids in daycare, and take the job at Sanchez's lounge. Brandon needed a wakeup call.

Earlier that morning Brandon was livid as Imani was preparing to awaken the boys for daycare so he'd picked an argument.

"Well, you know my mother is upstairs, and she's pretty upset that you went and put the boys in daycare. She loves them and has no problem keeping them," he said with a bit of an attitude.

Imani looked at Brandon with fury, "You and I are these kids' parents and I believe they should learn how to be around other kids their age. While I appreciate your parents, they won't be with us forever, so I'm just preparing now. I sure hope you explained that to your mother. Besides, she can get them on the weekends."

Brandon looked at Imani with annoyance and said, "Well I hope your black-ass know I ain't paying for it."

Those words and the tone in which he spoke, stopped her dead in her tracks. This was a first. They not only shocked her, but they cut her. Deep.

She had no idea of how or when it happened, but it was apparent; Brandon had turned into a man she no longer recognized. She wondered... *How did she go from being the black beauty that he wanted to marry, to becoming a black ass at that very moment?* That was verbal abuse, and she would not stand for that. He'd finally crossed the line.

Imani remained calm, and stepped right up to him, and put her finger in his face. She began to scorn him like he was a small child.

"Brandon, this was not how I envisioned our lives. I want what was promised to me in the beginning. I want the Brandon that I first met to resurface. He would have never talked to me like that. My parents have been together for close to thirty years, and I've never heard them say disrespectful things to each other, so I won't allow you to say those things to me. Now you need to apologize, right now!" She demanded.

Brandon didn't say a word. It was as if Imani wasn't there, because he continued playing his video game like a small child.

Imani repeated herself once more. Brandon still offered no response. He continued with his game, never considering her feelings.

Suddenly, Imani became frustrated and snatched the game controller from his hand. That got his attention fast. Brandon jumped up and said, "Quit playing and give me my controller. I'm in the middle of a game." He growled.

Imani held the controller over her head and yelled, "Not until you apologize."

Brandon was so angry, that he reached over her head, and grabbed both her wrists. "I don't owe you anything!" Imani tried to hold on to the controller, but his nails dug so deep inside her skin, it caused great pain. "Ouch!' she screamed, releasing the controller.

She looked at her wrists. They were bruised with several small cuts. "Look what you've done." She yelled.

He looked at the small cuts and said, "Oh you're so dramatic. Those are nothing but scratches, and it's not like I did it on purpose." He then said, "I'm sorry. Now, are you satisfied?"

Imani huffed, grabbed the twin's bags, and headed to their rooms. She spoke through tears, "Brandon, I appreciate everything your parents have done for us, and hopefully soon, the boys and I will be moving out on our own."

Brandon turned his attention back to his game, threw his hand up dismissively and said, "whatever."

ꟹ

Imani snapped back to reality and pushed that confrontation with Brandon to the back of her mind. She shoved her phone inside her bag. She began to rifle through the bag until she found her gift from LaShawn. It was a black satin pouch with a pink ribbon. Inside the pouch was a tube of lipstick, eyeshadow, a compact mirror and perfume. Frustrated, Imani headed straight to the bathroom.

She stared at herself in the mirror. Imani was thin, petite, with mocha colored skin tone, and shoulder length "boring hair" that was pulled up into a bun. She looked down at her clothes. The T-shirt with Sanchez lounge was oversized, and her leggings tended to sag a bit from her recent weight loss. Her rhinestone flip-flops were the only things she liked because they accented her perfect pedicure.

Imani stared back into the mirror. This time moving in a little closer to better examine herself. She never realized how much she looked like her mother, minus the vibrancy. She wanted to smile, but she couldn't.

Her mother was beautiful inside and out. What made her mother so attractive, had nothing to do with cosmetics, although she always dolled herself up. Her mother was beautiful because she was happy. Imani contributed most of her mother's happiness to the real "MVP" her father.

Imani decided to make a change. If it were only for a day, she would do something that she hadn't done in a long time, and that was to make herself feel good. Feel pretty. Feel alive.

She slipped inside the stall and removed the over-sized shirt and the saggy leggings. She took both hands and stretched the neck of the shirt outward. When she heard the first rip, she began to smile. She held it up. It suddenly looked like a dress to her. She giggled as she slipped on her new off the shoulders dress. She then let down that "boring" bun. Her hair fell flat, so she ran her fingers through it so that it could look a little fluffy.

Imani stepped over to the mirror and liked what she saw. But something was missing. She reached inside the satin pouch and pulled out the fresh tube of bright red lipstick. She dabbed a few spots on each cheek and rubbed it in. She giggled some more. It wasn't professional, but it was a start. She then closed her eye and ran a strip of lipstick across each lid, before tracing both her lips with the tube. She did have eyeshadow, and some other things in the bag, but she had no time to play with those. She had to get back to work.

Imani did a final once-over in the mirror. She was satisfied and liked what she saw.

Imani gathered the pouch, and the saggy leggings, and headed back out to the bar. She knew she had to change back into "boring" Imani after she left work. But, her mind was set; she'd make this a night to remember.

Imani hurried back to her post going unnoticed. The crowd was light, so she wasn't missed at all. She was nervous and needed something to calm herself. Imani then did something she'd never done before. She took the bottle of tequila and poured herself a double shot. Imani turned up what LaShawn called "liquid courage" and gulped it down in two swallows. It was strong and had a horrible taste, but after a few minutes, she understood why her friend called it that. Imani felt courageous.

She stooped under the bar to put her things away when she heard in a loud, cheerful voice, "Jack and coke please." She was startled. It was Mr. Sanchez's voice. She took several deep breaths, before slowly coming up for air. Although she was short, the tequila gave her confidence. She felt tall. Their eyes locked. Mr. Sanchez was transfixed. He put one hand up to his chest, "Oh, my goodness. How can this be?" He said stumbling over his words.

Imani cut him off while smiling and grinning. "What's wrong? You think it's a case of "Mistaken Identity?"

Imani stepped away and sashayed toward the liquor counter. She wanted him to have a full view, of the strange woman who was tending his bar. She poured his drink and set it directly in front of him. He couldn't help himself. "I never knew you had this in you. You are a beautiful *Black Goddess*," He said seeming almost mesmerized.

Imani let out a mischievous snicker. She'd heard those words all her life and once took them at face value. She believed that those words were a compliment and could lead to love like her parents had. But lately, hearing them bothered her. She owed that to Brandon.

Imani looked at Mr. Sanchez and said, "Thank you. You're not too bad looking yourself," she winked and flirted, deciding to turn her irritation into opportunity. Her look suddenly turned devious as she asked, "Now about that next vacation?"

Mr. Sanchez was flattered. "Whenever you want to go." He responded. He reached inside his wallet and handed her a hundred-dollar bill, along with a ten. "The ten is for the drink, and the rest is for you." Imani graciously accepted the tip. She slightly lowered her tattered dress, and seductively stuffed the bill inside.

Imani knew that she probably wouldn't take the vacation. She could never leave her boys. But it felt good to know that she still had it. She could still turn heads.

Besides, no one ever said that she couldn't dream, wish, or have a little fun; even if it were only for a day.

ଓ

The night had ended. The bar was nearly empty except for a few drunken patrons who lingered around laughing, joking and sharing old stories about the Vietnam War. The two waitresses didn't mind, because this was the most profitable part of the evening. The longer the men stayed, the heftier their tip jars became.

Imani was dead tired. She worked the opposite side of the bar, where there were no patrons. She'd re-stocked the refrigerator, loaded the glasses in the dishwasher, and wiped down the long counter with disinfectant. She was done for the evening.

She grabbed her personal belongings along with her tip jar, which overflowed with bills. She dumped the bills into her bag and sat the jar back on top of the bar. She'd been there for a little over a month, and this was the most she'd ever made in one night. She estimated it to be at least a couple hundred dollars. If she added the extra one-hundred-dollar tip from Mr. Sanchez, she'd almost have enough to take care of the past due daycare bill.

She looked down at her watch; it was fifteen after two in the morning. She knew she needed to hurry, as

Brandon would be waiting up for her. *Well, she didn't really believe he was actually waiting up for her.* That was the excuse he'd use as to why he was up playing the game so late.

Imani finally made it to the bathroom. When she glanced at herself in the mirror, she let out a pitiful laugh, as she looked an absolute mess. Her lipstick was smudged, her face was extra shiny, and her hair was matted and frizzy. Imani was soon reminded of why she never bothered to wear her hair down. She ran her hands through the water and dampened her hair as she pulled it back into a bun. She grabbed several pieces of paper towels and cleaned her face. She pulled the tattered shirt over her shoulders and slipped back into the leggings. She'd plan to run inside the house, and rip her clothes off, praying Brandon wouldn't notice. She was in no mood to continue the altercation from earlier.

When she exited the bathroom, she heard someone yell out her name. *"Oh boy!"* She said to herself; she really needed to get going. When she turned in the direction of the voice, it was Mr. Sanchez standing behind the bar, restocking the liquor. He smiled, as they made eye contact. He then nodded his head inviting her to join him.

She paused while letting out a heavy sigh. She knew she couldn't possibly ignore him. Although he was her boss, she'd never really held a private conversation with him before this evening, other than their initial interview.

Nervous, and consumed with self-doubt, she slowly moved forward, copping a seat directly in front of him. He handed her a folded piece of paper.

“These belong to you. I found them on the floor behind the bar.” He said in an empathetic tone.

Imani lowered her head as she opened the papers. She was embarrassed. It was her class schedule, along with the past due daycare bill. She sighed, as she rested her elbows on the bar and began to massage her temples, in an attempt to relieve some of the stress. She heard Mr. Sanchez pour something in a glass, but she couldn’t see what it was. He set it directly in front of her. “Looks like you could use this.” He whispered. Imani froze as she stared at the clear liquid.

Mr. Sanchez suddenly produced an envelope. “Here’s your pay.”

Imani was still trying to maintain her composure. It wasn’t payday so she accepted the money with a bit of trepidation. The envelope felt much heavier than usual. She only made ten bucks an hour. The extra fifty, he’d always thrown in, never really amounted to anything more than two hundred dollars. The tips are what kept her afloat.

In a shaky voice, she managed to speak. “Mr. Sanchez tomorrow is payday. Why would you pay me a day early?”

He gave a friendly smile. “Because I need you to do something for me.”

There was a long pause as she waited for him to complete the sentence. He never did. He looked as though he was searching for the right words to say. She suddenly began to feel slightly faint. Her heart palpitated at double the speed. She started to feel uneasy.

She stared at the thick package, then back up at Mr. Sanchez. She had no idea what he needed her to do, but she knew whatever it was, it didn’t sound good.

She lifted her arm attempting to hand the envelope back when he intervened. He gently grabbed her wrists and pushed them away. He refused to take no for an answer. That’s when he felt them — *the cuts.* They were small and tiny, but they were there. He no longer wore the smile. A look of concern replaced it. “What happened to your wrists?”

Imani was ashamed, so she snatched away. She could have easily said one of the twins scratched her, but that would have been a lie. *She didn’t like to lie.* In an attempt to thwart the attention from her injured wrists, Imani opened the envelope. Her eyes tripled in size as she counted twelve crisp fifty-dollar bills. She suddenly felt nauseous. Things seemed to be going from bad to worse. She was now in a state of confusion. Speechless. Seemingly locked into a bad dream.

“*Oh my goodness, what have I gotten myself into?*” She thought to herself. She immediately regretted her actions from earlier. The hair, the dress, the lipstick; was all a façade. Stupid. Now Mr. Sanchez probably viewed her as a piece of property that could easily be bought and sold. She thought about her tips. Her hands began to shake. She tried to remain at ease, but even that was becoming difficult. She contemplated dumping the entire bag, with all her earnings on the counter, and running out the door never to return.

She and LaShawn often teased about how good Mr. Sanchez looked. "Mr. Sanchez is fine as hell for his age. I bet he had women falling all over him when he was younger." She'd joke and laugh. But at the moment, it's no laughing matter.

Mr. Sanchez was once a professional golfer; now he did it for pleasure. He was of medium height, with an athletic build, short, salt, and pepper hair with light brown eyes, and a sandy brown tan. Although he was undeniably handsome for his age, Mr. Sanchez was too old for her. There was no way that she could even consider the possibility of dating a man that was old enough to be her father.

She'd been keeping up with the current events in the news, and she now understood what "*sexual harassment*" in the workplace was all about. She wondered would the rules apply to her if she were forced to sleep with her boss. She questioned if she had brought this on herself. She thought she was only having a little fun. She wanted to look and feel pretty. She wanted to pretend if only for a day, she was someone else. Most of all, she wanted attention. But for her, this was a bit much. She'd never in a million years think it would lead to this.

"Imani?" Mr. Sanchez softly called. His voice startled her. She quickly gasped for breath. He handed her the drink, and on impulse, she grabbed it. Imani braced herself as she took a huge gulp. On reflex, she immediately spat it out. Her mind was prepared for the strong taste of alcohol, but instead, it was just water.

Mr. Sanchez grabbed a few napkins to clean up the mess. "What's wrong, did it go down the wrong pipe?" he asked out of concern. She looked up and felt like a silly child. She had to pull it together. This was wrong on so many levels, and she had to fix it.

She sealed the envelope and handed it back to Mr. Sanchez. "I…I.. can't accept this. This…this isn't right."

He cut her off. "Please, let me explain." Although she had her mind made up, she decided to let him say whatever it was he had to say. She also knew that it would most likely be her last day working for Mr. Sanchez.

He stared deep into her eyes. She wanted to look away, but for some strange reason, she was drawn to him. Warmth, concern, and compassion were the energy his eyes gave. A guilty chill washed upon her as he said sternly. "Imani, I gave you that money because, I need for you to never, ever, pull that stunt again. I mean never!" He reiterated.

She was shocked and frozen still.

"I need you to keep all of your clothes on because that's not a good look for you." He said firmly.

Imani felt as though her ears were deceiving her. But they were not. Her heart suddenly plunged to the pit of her stomach as she tried her best to hold back the tears. *She didn't even have what it took to turn an old man on, and for that, she felt like a complete fool.*

Mr. Sanchez pointed to the opposite side of the bar. "Look at Jasmine, and Destiny over there."

Oh wow! Imani thought. She could never compete with them. Next, to LaShawn, they were also top waitresses in the bar. Jasmine was gorgeous. She had a friendly smile, beautiful hair, and a shapely figure. Imani couldn't ever recall a time when Jasmine didn't look runway ready. Destiny didn't exactly have a killer body, but she had huge DD breasts to make-up for whatever she lacked. Destiny loved putting the "twins" on display. She was loud, boisterous, and personable, but she had no filter. Whatever came up, came out, and that's exactly why most of the customers loved her.

Jasmine and Destiny, both leaned over the bar wearing tank tops exposing their assets. They smiled and laughed, as they conversed with the three older gentlemen pretending to care while racking up their tip jars. *They were so good at this game.*

Mr. Sanchez said, "Please don't take this the wrong way, but I hire folks for different reasons." He let out a charming smile, "I believe they have that department covered." He didn't give her a chance to sulk. "Imani, I hired you for your beautiful spirit and your innocence. I liked you because you didn't look like them. Your natural beauty is enough. Besides you don't have much back there, or up top anyway."

That statement seemed to ease all the tension. "They both let out a hearty, laugh, and Imani was finally able to exhale. Imani sipped the glass of water and swallowed it along with her pride as he continued to speak.

☙

I came to America from Puerto Rico as a young child. My father came first. We were very poor. The reason we were able to make it was because we had help from other's who'd come before us. They helped my father with housing and finding a job in the steel factory. My father was able to send for my mother, and me along with my siblings. He taught me that if you were ever in a position to help someone, do it. "For it is far greater to give, than it is to receive."

As a young boy, my father brought home an old pair of golf clubs that one of his co-workers was discarding. He gave them to me. I played with those things and played with those things until I became good at it. Those clubs changed my life. They sent me to college on an athletic scholarship, and after college, golf became my profession. I won many tournaments and became a very wealthy man because of it.

I met my beautiful wife Mary Ann at one of those tournaments, and a few years later we had three lovely daughters. My wife never had to work, and I was able to help my father retire, and start this business. If it wasn't for my father's co-worker giving me those golf clubs, I might have never found my true gift.

Imani, when I interviewed you, I saw my beautiful wife, Mary Ann. She was the most exceptional woman a man like me could ever have. I can only hope that your boyfriend appreciates what he has. Back when I first started, I'd play at those golf tournaments, and so many beautiful women would throw themselves at me. I could get a woman quicker than I could order a drink. I'd always be flattered, but I wanted something that was real, genuine, and everlasting like my parents had. Mary Ann was exactly that. What made her that was the fact that she never threw herself at me. I had to earn her love and respect. She treated me like a regular customer instead of this big shot that those other women made me out to be. That's what drew me to her. Even after I married her, she never changed, and I believe I fell in love with her more and more because of it. I just loved that beautiful, strong woman. I chased after that woman, and loved on that woman, up until the day she took her last breath. Although she told me she loved me every day, she always kept me guessing and on my toes. I bought her roses every week up until the day she died. She didn't make me do it either. I wanted to do it. I believe some women have that special gift, the gift to have men falling in love with them well after they've landed him. Imani, you have that same gift. Please don't ever sell yourself short.

☙

Hearing this caused Imani to drop her head, losing all the ability to speak. She rubbed her scarred wrist and began to weep. She didn't feel the tears coming. They caught her off guard. She guessed she'd suppressed the truth for so long. She was overwhelmed, miserable, and confused. She loved Brandon but didn't feel as though that love was reciprocated. Lately, the only thing that kept her going was her twin boys, Nelson and Martin.

Imani took several deep breaths as she gathered her things. Mr. Sanchez tried to comfort her, but it was no use. Suffocating in her own sorrow, she knew she had to get out of there.

She managed to thank him right before dashing out the door.

☙

Imani cranked the ignition to the Jeep and sat there for a few minutes to let the car idle. When she noticed the time and realized Brandon hadn't called, she contemplated sending him a more in-depth message by not going home at all. Since she'd never stayed away from home before, she was sure that would get his attention. The fear of losing her would have to make him get his act together.

She thought of renting a hotel room, but she really couldn't afford it. She thought of going to her parent's home but quickly decided against that. They had already done so much for her and the boys. Besides, she still loved Brandon, and running home to her parents would only complicate things even more.

Imani knew that her father didn't much care for Brandon; he only tolerated him. In his eyes, Brandon was just a grown child. His parents were wealthy, and he had it too easy.

Mr. McNair never forgot the time that Brandon's car caught a flat outside of their home, and he had no clues, as to how to fix it. Brandon called his father, and his father's solution was to call a towing service. Imani's father stepped in and told Allen Garrison he'd handle it. Mr. McNair explained to Brandon as gently as he possibly could on how a man should always have a basic set of tools, he should be able to do small repairs, as well as know-how to change a flat tire. Mr. McNair proceeded to show Brandon what to do, but Brandon was disinterested, and this bothered Mr. McNair. He was not angry that he didn't know how to change the flat; he was more disappointed in the fact Brandon didn't care to know.

That situation left a bad impression on Mr. McNair, one that he would never forget. Peter McNair had learned how to change a flat tire well before he knew how to drive. He couldn't imagine what would have happened, if Imani and the kids were with him on the road, and they caught a flat. Sure, Brandon and his family had money; but Peter McNair knew, that money didn't make you a man.

Although he didn't have the type of money that the Garrison's had, he had enough money to buy his daughter an older model Jeep at an auction. He wanted her to have her own. He put a rebuilt engine in it, along with new tires, and gave it a fresh paint job. The expression on Imani's face was priceless when he presented it to her as a gift. He loved his daughter with all his heart. It tore him apart to think that she'd run off and start a family so young; in hopes of catapulting her way to the top, without putting in the real hard work.

Peter McNair knew that his daughter and Brandon's relationship was on borrowed time. He saw how motherhood made her more mature when Brandon stayed the same. Whenever Imani came over to visit, he noticed how she no longer had that sparkle in her eyes; it had been replaced by weariness.

ℭ𝔅

The tears flowed uninterrupted as Imani pulled the Jeep onto the main road. She knew that her obligation was to her children, so she was left with no choice but to go home.

She entered the subdivision, surveying all the big beautiful homes. Some had circular drives, accented by perfect landscaping, decorative lighting, and tall trees. She remembered being in awe coming here for the first time. She couldn't believe one kid had all this growing up. She had to admit that her attraction to him grew deeper because of it.

She envisioned her and Brandon owning a home of their own. She wanted the very best for their children. She wanted them to have all the things that she didn't, including a room of their own. But those dreams that she once shared with Brandon were soon fading. He just wasn't ready to grow up. As long as his parents held the safety net, Brandon saw no need to grow up.

The motion lights lit up as she entered the driveway. Brandon would usually meet her outside just as she'd pull into the four-car garage. That day he didn't. This angered her even further.

She pulled into her designated spot and slammed the truck door as she exited the vehicle. She fumbled around in her purse, for the keys. When she finally made it inside the house, she was pissed at what she saw. Brandon sat in front of the TV, laughing, and joking, wearing his video headphones, oblivious to her presence. It was after three o'clock in the morning, and the house was in utter chaos. Trails of cereal, crumbled up graham crackers, fruit snacks, and juice boxes were scattered around the room. Shoes and clothes were in the middle of the floor along with shredded pieces of paper.

She dropped her bag and headed to the twin's room. Their room was nice and tidy, but they weren't there. She stormed into the room she shared with Brandon. She became even angrier at what she found. It was as if a hurricane had hit the place. Every article of clothing that she owned was on the floor. Her shoes were scattered all over the room, her college book bag had been emptied, and her notebooks had been scribbled on.

This is one of the reasons the kids needed daycare she thought to herself. He was so irresponsible when it came to watching them.

She began to clear the king size bed. She just knew that they'd fell asleep under all the mess they'd made. To her surprise, they weren't there.

She stormed out of the room and ran over to the TV and yanked the headphones from the socket. She then snatched the game controller from his hand. The loud voices were now coming through the TV speakers.

Brandon jumped up, "What the hell is your problem?"

Imani suddenly heard a voice say through the speakers, "Woooo!" Imani ignored it.

She yelled at Brandon, "Where the hell are my kids?"

Brandon became incensed because she'd interrupted his game. "Well they're my kids too." He yelled back.

Imani's breathing was at an uncontrollable rate as she asked the question again. This time she added more bass, "I said, where the hell are my kids?"

Brandon finally responded, "My mother came down and got them. They're leaving for Traverse city early in the morning." He said furiously.

Still not satisfied, Imani continued to yell through the tears, "Well why did you sit here and let them tear the house up like this? Brandon, this is unacceptable. You are such a big kid, and you need to grow up!" She said in inflammatory anger.

Being called a kid infuriated Brandon. His chest swelled up as his breathing began to match hers. "Well you're too damn grown, and probably should take it down a few notches." He retorted. "My Mom and Dad already raised me, so I suggest you stick to mothering the twins because I don't need a parent. As far as your stuff being thrown all over the room, well I did that. I couldn't find your suitcases, but then I remembered - you didn't come with any." He responded angrily.

Laughter suddenly came through the TV speakers. A soft female voice spoke. "Brandon, I'll call you later. It seems as though you have your hands full."

Caught off guard, they both stared at the TV. Imani expected many things from Brandon, but never anything like this. She glared at him and couldn't help but to notice guilt written all over his face. He was busted.

Imani was hurt and became enraged. For the first time, she lost total control. The number one rule her father gave her and her sisters when it came to relationships went out the window. "Never lay your hands on a man and never challenge his manhood." He preached this to them their entire lives. "Ladies, no matter how hard you try or how angry you become, you can't whip a man." Those words meant nothing to her at that second. Brandon had indeed crossed the line. She was ready for war.

Her eyes became huge, she clenched both her hands turning them into tight fists, and she took a deep breath before she let it out. "You bastard. How could you?" She completely lost it. Imani ducked her head and began to violently swing both her arms in windmill fashion as fast and as hard as she could. Each blow landed on Brandon's chest. She was angry, so she fought through the heartache, the pain, and the tears. She fought for the lost years, the untruths, and the deceit. But more than anything she fought because she was lost, confused, and soon to be thrown into a world, in which she was ill-prepared. Brandon knew better than to hit her back; however, he couldn't just stand there and do nothing. He was finally able to catch both her wrist. He shook her in an attempt to take control of the situation.

"Imani? Stop it! This relationship has been over for a while, and you know it! After we had the twins, you changed. You stopped being fun. You became demanding and controlling, and you stopped taking care of yourself. We're both still young, and there's no reason that we have to give up everything just because we're parents."

Imani didn't hear a word he said; she only wanted to know one thing. "Who the hell is she?"

She wasn't expecting an answer. She was expecting him to lie or try to cover it up. But he did neither. He responded, "She's someone who knows how to have fun and not act like my mother. She's someone who doesn't take life so seriously, she accepts me for me, and she loves the kids and video games."

Imani came to a complete halt. The fact that he hadn't denied the mystery woman, and the fact that he took her around their children enraged Imani all over again. She began kicking, and screaming, and losing complete control all over again.

Brandon shoved her away and yelled, "I'm leaving. I will not fight you." I did everything in my power to try and please you, but it seems it's just not good enough. So, I quit trying."

Brandon went on to say, "When I finished school and was promoted to manager at Game Stop, you said I needed to find a more professional job. When I dress the kids, you say those aren't the clothes that you set out for them to wear. When I bought them a video game, you said the kids shouldn't play with those types of games. When my dad bought my graduation present, and I chose to get a Dodge Challenger, instead of a minivan, you almost lost your mind."

Imani was so hurt and couldn't believe her ears. They started out on the same road, but somewhere along the way, she'd lost him. He'd taken another turn. With tears still streaming down her face, and trying desperately to control her breathing, she said as calmly as she possibly could, "So you mean to tell me that the wedding, buying our own home, and building a future together is all over, because I'm growing and you're not ready or willing to do the same?"

Brandon knew he was being berated, so he stopped her in her tracks. "Imani, We're too young for all of this. My father was right; I'm not ready for marriage."

Imani squinted her teary eyes at him as she picked her heart up off the floor. That was it. She was out of there.

"Screw you, Brandon! I'll leave. I'm going to show you better than I can tell you. I don't need you."

She ran to the kitchen to grab some garbage bags. When she looked around, she sure was going to miss the place. The Garrison's put state of the art furniture throughout the home. The kitchen was spacious with granite counter tops, beautiful ceramic floors, nice oak cabinets, and stainless steel appliances. It also had a large family room, an office, and there was a bathroom in each of the two bedrooms. But Imani had to let it go, none of that mattered. It wasn't hers, and because she wasn't married to him, it would never be hers. She had no rights to anything.

She grabbed the garbage bags and packed as much stuff as she possibly could. She didn't bother with packing all the kids' things. His parents loved them too much, and there was no way she would use them as leverage. They would have to work out some sort of agreement. She wanted nothing from Brandon. She wanted to show him that she could make it on her own.

☙

Her parents' home was dark and looked deserted. She didn't want to disturb them at four o'clock in the morning, but she was officially homeless. She had no choice. She rang the bell once. If they didn't answer, she'd sleep in the car until the morning.

About a minute later, the porch lit up. Both of her parents peeked frantically through the window. Mr. McNair snatched the door open once he saw her sad face. Her parents asked in a concerned tone, "Is everything alright?"

Imani couldn't help but notice their attire. Her mother's hair was wild, and she had on a beautiful short satin nightgown with the robe to match. Her father wore satin pajama bottoms, with a ribbed tank top, and black slippers. The one thing she knew about her parents, was that they were definitely in love. They had always been affectionate with each other, and she felt terrible, because from the look of things she had disturbed what seemed like a special evening.

She tried not to, but she couldn't help herself. She fell into her father's arms and burst into full-blown tears. "Brandon and I are over, and I didn't have anywhere else to go."

Her father's natural response was, "What? You mean to tell me he put you out at four o'clock in the morning?" He started searching for his shoes. " Wait till I get my hands on him. I'm going to teach that coward a lesson."

Her mother took control, "Pete, stop it! You're not leaving this house."

Imani sat down on her parents' couch, the same couch in which she was chastened when she was a young girl experiencing make-up for the first time. Her mother listened and suspended judgment, but her father, on the other hand, did not.

He was angry and didn't hold anything back. "Imani, I knew that relationship wasn't going to work. I tried to stay out of it for as long as I could, but he's forced my hand. When I get home from work this evening, we're going straight over there to get you and the twins things. You're coming back home with us, and that's final!" He said before storming toward the stairs.

Imani bowed her head. This was the very reason she didn't want to come here. Her father was too demanding and controlling. Imani believed that she was a responsible adult, but the way that her father spoke to her, left room for doubt.

Mrs. McNair could sense Imani's sadness. "Pete, if hindsight were 20/20 then no one would ever learn. We'd all be perfect and free of mistakes. We must be supportive of her and help her in any way we can. She doesn't need this right now."

Her father stopped midway up the stairs and yelled, "I know exactly what she needs, and that's to come back home and this is not up for debate. Imani, be here when I get home from work!" He yelled before disappearing up the stairs.

Her mother shrugged her shoulders and hugged her. She stepped over to the closet and retrieved some clean blankets. “Right now, you can sleep here on the couch. In the morning, your brothers will be home from camp, and I’ll have them clean up your old room. As long as your father and I are alive, you and the boys have a place to stay.”

ଓ

Sleep wouldn’t come easy. Imani tossed, turned, and cried while staring at the ceiling on the small couch. The large grandfather clock in the corner let her know that only forty minutes had passed. She replayed what happened an hour earlier in her mind. She couldn’t stop thinking of the hurtful things Brandon had said. *“You let yourself go.”* had been the worst.

How could a man berate a woman for putting her children’s needs before her own? Wasn’t that how it was supposed to work?

Imani thought of that *“Fix my life”* lady, Iyanla Vanzant. Her mother watched her all the time. Imani wondered if she could call her for Brandon only; *because her life wasn’t the one broken.*

Before Imani had children, she’d always kept herself up. She had been going to LaShawn’s to have her hair done at least twice a week since high school. When her children were smaller, Imani looked forward to spending time with LaShawn at the salon while Brandon sat at home with the kids. It gave her a much-needed break. But in the process of doing her hair, LaShawn would stop, and take breaks, talk on the phone, try on clothes, eat a snack, smoke a cigarette, dance, and even run to the store. But when her children started getting older, Imani no longer had that sort of time. So, having her hair professionally styled was the last thing on her priority list.

Imani liked being a "hands-on" parent. Seeing her children happy made her happy. You could easily find her at the park playing in the sand with the boys, in the backyard playing on their swing set, or she'd even take them swimming at the beach. When the day would come to an end, she'd always look a mess so Imani found it easier to pull her hair up into a bun, slip on a pair of leggings and a t-shirt, and keep it moving. Unless she and Brandon were going out on a date, she didn't bother with clothes. As Imani continued to think about it; they hadn't been on an actual date in months. She began to weep again.

Imani rose from the couch to get some water. Maybe that would help her sleep.

The small kitchen was a few feet away from the living room. Imani opened the fridge and grabbed a bottle of water and sat at the kitchen table. She looked around the room. It was small. In fact, the entire house was small. Imani then realized that the house was not big enough figuratively and literally for her and Peter

McNair. She understood that if she came back home, she'd be voluntarily relinquishing all her rights as an adult and she'd run the risk of being treated like a small child. Being back at her parents and sleeping on their couch made her realize just how far she hadn't come. Although she loved them deeply, there was no way she could move back home, even if it were only temporary.

"Imani soon realized that she was much too big, for the small world in which she had come."

Imani finally dozed off. The ringing of her cellphone around eight o'clock in the morning jarred her awake. She was tired, drained and disoriented. The caller ID let her know it was Brandon's mother, Mrs. Garrison.

"Good Morning Imani," She said candidly. "We'll be leaving to head up north in a little over an hour. I was wondering if you were coming by to see the boys off before we leave?"

Imani hesitated before she answered her question, she didn't quite know how to respond. She wondered if she should stay away from the house a little longer until things settled, but most of all, Imani wondered if she knew.

The Garrison's owned a large cottage along with a boat up in Traverse City, Michigan. Two weeks out of the year, Brandon's half-brothers along with their wives, their children, and other family members, would join them and they'd have one big grand old time.

"*Traverse City is approximately 255 miles away from Detroit, and the place is a great tourist attraction. It was voted as one of America's most charming towns. With about 180 miles of beautiful beaches, numerous wineries, eateries, small shops and Imani's personal favorite, The National Cherry Festival, it's a must-see*.

The past few years, the Garrison's started taking the twins with them for the two weeks. Brandon and Imani would join them the last weekend, where they'd have a big summer party. Imani became glum because she didn't believe that she would attend this year.

"Um, Mrs. Garrison I'm at my parents' house, so you'll have to give me about a half an hour." Mrs. Garrison pleasantly responded, "Ok dear. I'll see you then."

Imani reached inside her bag and retrieved a pair of sweats, a t-shirt, and a baseball cap. The sweats and t-shirt were wrinkled, but she had no time to iron. She made her way to the bathroom and freshened up. When she looked in the mirror, her eyes were still puffy and red from crying. She ran a hot rag under the water and placed them on her eyes. The steam from the cloth was soothing.

As she exited the bathroom, Ms. McNair was descending the top of the stairs. “Imani, where are you going? I was going to fix some breakfast?”

Imani avoided all eye contact. She didn’t want her mother to see her puffy face, but most of all she didn’t want the sympathy. She hurriedly brushed past her mother heading to the door.

“Thanks, mom, but I’m not hungry. I have to head home to see the twins off. Mr. and Mrs. Garrison are taking them up north for two weeks, for their annual trip.”

When she called the Garrison’s place her home, her mother gave her a disturbed look. Imani immediately began to explain herself, trying her best to backpedal her actions from earlier. “Mom, it was just a small spat. I came here because I needed to get some air. Brandon and I will fix this.”

Mrs. McNair wore a look of disappointment after she’d realized her daughter was not moving back home. She extended her arms and embraced Imani. “You know that you’re going to hear from your father?” She whispered in her ear.

“I know,” Imani said as she reciprocated her mother’s embrace.

Imani reached for her belongings, popped the baseball cap on her head, and headed out the door.

Imani had made up her mind; she was going back home to Brandon. Maybe with the kids being away for two weeks, she and Brandon could try and rekindle what they once had. She'd plan to call LaShawn once she returned from her trip later in the day. Imani wanted to treat herself to a full makeover. She had too much at stake to throw in the towel. She decided that she would fight for what was hers.

ଓ

There was a white windowless van with the words "Howard the handyman" parked in the middle of the driveway. Imani was forced to park on the street. When she made it to the door, it was open. A burly black man wearing coveralls splattered with dried paint, a baseball cap, and dusty boots, blocked the entrance.

The Garrison's home was beautiful and immaculate. Imani couldn't imagine what type of work that needed to be done. But she knew Mrs. Garrison. She loved beautiful things. So it was no big deal for her to hang a new light fixture or wall art, or merely move furniture around.

The gentleman handed Mrs. Garrison a white envelope and said, "your son has instructed me to leave this with you." Mrs. Garrison accepted the envelope and smiled at the gentleman as they both exchanged good-byes.

Imani silently stood as he opened the screen door and exited the home. Mrs. Garrison, who was wearing a pink nylon-jogging suit, with a white shirt and clean white canvas shoes, finally noticed her standing there. Imani began to feel uncomfortable as Mrs. Garrison stared at her with a look of pity, seeming to be at a loss for words. Imani looked down at her ragged attire and understood why. The woman was a perfectionist, and she was not.

Once again, she was haunted by Brandon's words. "You let yourself go." Imani made a promise to herself that she would never leave out of the house looking that way ever again.

After several seconds of silence, Mrs. Garrison smiled and said, "I'm glad you made it dear, "the boys are in the game room." Imani removed her shoes and headed to see the boys.

The twins sat on the couch in front of the oversize flat screen television. The Disney channel seemed to be watching them because they were engrossed in playing the hand-held video games that Brandon had recently purchased for them. They never noticed her standing there.

She called out to them. "Martin. Nelson. Mom's here. Can I have a hug?" She said in an upbeat voice.

The rambunctious boys dropped their video games and ran to give her a tight hug. She closed her eyes and kissed the top of their foreheads cherishing the moment. Thoughts of walking away from her relationship with Brandon were no longer an option. It wasn't about what she wanted. Her boys deserved both of their parents, and she vowed to fight to the bitter end, to make sure that happened.

She embraced the boys one last time and said, "I need for you both to be good for your grandparents and make sure you brush your teeth and say your prayers before bed."

"We will mommy," they said in unison as they freed themselves from her embrace eager to get back to playing their video games.

Mrs. Garrison was in the kitchen filling the teapot with water when Imani interrupted. "Mrs. Garrison, in case I haven't told you, I appreciate everything you and your husband do for my family. Now, do you need me to go downstairs and get anything else for the boys?" Imani said.

Mrs. Garrison suddenly stopped what she was doing, and faced Imani with a perplexed look on her face. Imani knew right then, Brandon had told her what transpired between them early this morning. Mrs. Garrison let out a long sympathetic sigh and said, "Have a seat dear."

Imani began to feel nervous. She didn't want to have this discussion with his mother. Since she and Brandon had been living together, it seemed as though both their parents wanted to control every aspect of their lives when she and Brandon were in fact adults. At least she considered herself to be one.

However, Imani would be respectful and listen. That didn't mean that she had to accept whatever it was Mrs. Garrison had to say.

Mrs. Garrison sat two cups of tea on the table. She sipped her drink, but Imani was in no mood for any. She had more important things to do, like winning her man back.

"Imani, my husband has begged me to stay out of you and Brandon's business, and I promised him I would. So, what I'm about to say to you will be brief, and I hope that you don't take this the wrong way."

Imani looked at her, thinking to herself, *if only you had minded your business a long time ago, she and Brandon would probably be happily married.*

Imani believed that they were the problem. They were always there for Brandon. They solved all of his problems, never letting him figure things out for himself. Imani knew they loved the grandkids; she just wished they'd tell Brandon "no" when he needed a sitter. It wasn't fair that she was doing her part as a mother, and they were doing Brandon's part as a father.

But what was most important to Imani at the very moment was Mrs. Garrison sticking to the promise she'd made to her husband. Of course, she couldn't possibly say this, so Imani gave a meek smile, held her breath, and carefully listened as she spoke.

"Imani, I have watched you and my son throughout the years, and you two are wonderful parents. I don't believe that I can say this enough." Mrs. Garrison said.

Imani's heart rate began to speed as she braced herself for the caveat that she was sure would follow.

"But you my dear, have blossomed into this beautiful young woman that I barely recognize. As far as my son; I just wish I could say the same." Mrs. Garrison said with an odd look on her face.

"Boom!" There it was, Imani said to herself as she was starting to stand. She was not going to sit around while his mother bashed her man/ her son when she was one of the main persons who contributed to the problem.

Mrs. Garrison looked at her sternly forcing Imani to sit back down.

"Imani, you are more woman than you even realize. You are so far ahead of my son until I'm afraid, it will probably take him ten years to catch up. He's not ready for what you want- today, tomorrow or even next year. You've been so busy trying to turn him into something that he is not until you forget to take care of you physically." She said judgmentally.

Imani looked down at her wrinkled clothes, and touched her baseball cap and felt embarrassed as Mrs. Garrison continued.

"When I was your age, I walked in the same shoes as you minus the children. I had a modeling career at an early age, and with all the money I made, and the fancy things that I was able to buy, I was still searching for love. I chased after men I thought I loved, played silly games, and pleaded with them to act right. It wasn't until I understood my value that I stopped chasing those men and they started chasing me. What you fail to understand is that women mature much faster than men. So, in reality, you probably have my son by at least five years. Think about it; it's no coincidence that my husband is five years older than me." She said.

Imani looked at her confused. She believed that Mrs. Garrison had it all wrong. Imani didn't think that she was chasing Brandon; she thought she'd already had him. Mrs. Garrison noticed the puzzled look on Imani's face, so she was left with no choice but to spell it out for her.

"Imani when you got that job and put my grandchildren in daycare, I saw right through it. I knew what you were trying to do. You wanted him to step up, become more responsible, and shame him into becoming this perfect man and father overnight. But Imani I'm afraid that he never noticed, but I did." She said tenderly.

Imani felt ashamed. His mother had called her out. Mrs. Garrison wasn't trying to hurt her feelings, but these were things she felt Imani needed to hear. Mrs. Garrison reached across the table for her purse. She grabbed her checkbook and filled it out. She handed it to Imani.

"Take this check and take care of that daycare bill and use the rest to take care of yourself. I want you to get back to you. Please don't worry about the children; we will continue to support them for as long as we're on this earth and long after we're gone. It's nothing you can do about it either." She smiled.

Imani accepted the check. She never looked at the amount. That didn't matter. She was grateful for anything that she'd received.

She folded the check in half and tucked it inside her wallet. They both stood. Mrs. Garrison gave her a loving embrace. "Imani, please use these two weeks wisely. You deserve it."

Imani responded, "Thank-you Mrs. Garrison, but I'm not giving up on my relationship with Brandon. He may be a little behind, but I will learn to be patient. I'm going to do everything I absolutely can to make sure we get back on the same page."

Imani headed toward the door, "I'm going to go down and clean the place up, make a wonderful dinner, and I can assure you that Brandon and I will be up North, for your big summer party."

Mrs. Garrison's eyes and mouth became wide. She then pointed to the envelope given to her by the man in the white truck. She tried to speak, "But Brandon…"

Imani quickly cut her off and said as nicely as she possibly could, "Mrs. Garrison there are no but's. This is between Brandon and me. I really think it's time that you listened to your husband, and stay out of this, because I got this. Trust me. I got this."

Imani headed out the door, leaving Mrs. Garrison speechless and flummoxed.

☙

Imani was famished; as she couldn't remember the last time she had eaten. She had very little energy and had to get something on her stomach before she could even attempt to clean the house. She headed out to her Jeep, and before she reached the corner, she spotted Mr. Garrison driving his RV. He looked at her waving and smiling, as he honked his horn.

Mr. Garrison was a friendly man who loved his toys. They had motor homes, boats, snowmobiles, bikes, mopeds and any other toy one could think of. He believed in living life to the fullest.

Imani sat at the Coney Island restaurant and ordered the big breakfast. She thought about the condition of the house when she left it this morning and knew that it would take most of the day to clean it.

As Imani waited on her breakfast, she dialed LaShawn. LaShawn answered right away, full of energy and full of jokes.

"Hey Imani girl, you never call me this early unless it's about Brandon. What'd he do this time?" Imani laughed nervously. LaShawn knew her all too well, for they'd been friends way too long.

Imani tried as best as she could to sound positive. "Oh, nothing. The twins are gone for two weeks, and Brandon is at work. I figured I'd come and let you do my hair and we could have some girl time."

LaShawn couldn't be fooled that easily. She knew that an early phone call from Imani meant that she needed her. So instead of badgering her any further, she responded with, "Um hmnnn sure. Just let me get home, and get myself unpacked and settled, and we can shoot for four o'clock."

Imani felt relieved that she was no longer under the microscope. She ended with, "Thank you bestie, I'll see you soon."

☙

Imani still needed to buy some time. She wanted to make sure that the Garrison's were well on the road before she returned so she stopped at the local drugstore a few blocks away from the house. She wanted the evening with Brandon to be perfect. She grabbed a bottle of wine, candles, body spray, lip-gloss, garbage bags, window cleaner, and bleach.

When she finally made it to the house, she was happy to find that there were no cars in the driveway, the blinds were closed, and the home was secure.

Once Imani parked her Jeep in the driveway, she grabbed the bags from the drugstore and set them by the door. She walked back to the truck and grabbed the garbage bags with her things. As she pulled the heavy bags, the plastic stretched and began to wear thin. She was so happy that she wouldn't have to make this trip again. It was such a nuisance. Once she finally got a good grip on the bag, it burst open, leaving all her belongings scattered in the driveway. "*Oh well, one more thing to add to her cleaning list.*" She whispered to herself.

Imani bent over and pushed all her things closer to the door. She was now exhausted and couldn't wait to soak in their large water jet tub without any interruptions.

As she inserted her key into the lock, her heart thumped when the key didn't turn. *"Calm down Imani; you're moving too fast.*" She whispered to herself. She tried to relax as she inserted the key again. It still didn't work. She was becoming emotional. Her eyes were puddled with tears as she tried every key on her ring; nothing worked.

Her mind flashed back to the handyman, Mrs. Garrison, and the envelope he had given to her from Brandon. It all made sense. "The locks had been changed." "That bastard!" She screamed.

Imani's feelings were hurt, and she could barely breathe. Her body began to weaken and out of nowhere, she burst into tears. She turned her back to the side of the house and placed her hands over her eyes to catch the sobs. She slowly slid down the side of the house landing on top of her pile of clothes. "Damn!" She yelled. "I don't need this right now." Her hopes for a fairytale life had finally ended. She looked back over the years and was filled with much regret. She sacrificed everything only to be left with nothing in the end.

Imani took a deep breath. She could no longer lie to herself. She was part of the blame. She liked the independence his parents provided for them. She loved being on her own, even if it were just an apartment in their basement. When her parents tried to reason with her, she wouldn't listen.

She thought of the conversation she had with Mrs. Garrison earlier, and she finally had to agree. Imani indeed put Brandon's needs ahead of her own. She allowed him to go to school full time while she sat out for a year, to be there for their kids. She washed, cooked, and cleaned while he worked and played the video game. She became angrier as she thought of how the arrangement was fine until she decided to get a job and do something more with her life.

Imani sat there for the next few minutes and sobbed, and sobbed until she finally made herself stop. She managed to stand. She began to sift through all her things and found the garbage bags that she had just purchased. She ripped the box open and removed two bags. She grabbed the wine and sat it on her front seat. She then stuffed the rest of her belongings in the back of her truck.

She turned the ignition, slammed the gear into reverse and headed to Brandon's job.

☙

For Imani, everything was just a blur. She didn't know how she safely made it to Brandon's job in one piece. She'd broken the speed limit, ran red lights and blew past a few stop signs, making it there in records time.

Imani sped through the parking lot of the plaza, which housed a Game Stop, coffee shop, fitness center, and several small boutiques. She slowed down once she'd noticed two police officers, one male and the other female, heading inside the coffee shop. Imani quickly spotted Brandon's shiny, black, on black, Dodge Challenger and parked directly next to it. She purposely flung her car door open wide, leaving a deep indentation on the passenger side door. She felt satisfied. Brandon loved and cherished that car, and she knew that he'd be torn up, once he detected the damage.

She pulled her baseball cap tightly over her head and rushed towards the Game stop. She passed a few gym goers, a few children, an elderly couple, and the young girl Erica, a new employee at Brandon's store. Imani contemplated asking Erica if she'd seen Brandon, but Erica was standing next to a black Ford Focus, facing the opposite way.

The bell chimed as Imani entered the store. The store was relatively empty except for a few children playing video games. Justin, who was an employee at the store, stood behind the counter with his back turned. He appeared to be organizing the video games.

"Hey Justin, is Brandon in?" Imani casually asked. Justin stopped sorting the videos and turned to face Imani. The nervous look in his eyes let her know that she'd caught him off guard.

Justin called out to a younger looking employee who'd just come from the back.

"Hey, Marvin, is Brandon in the back?" Justin asked with a slight tremor in his voice.

Imani stood there with her arms folded. She knew Justin, he and Brandon were good friends, but she'd never met the other guy.

Marvin responded very casually, “He stepped out for a few minutes to help Erica with something.” Justin tried his best to interrupt the young man, but it was too late. Imani had heard enough.

Brandon often spoke of Erica, a new employee who was fresh out of high school. Imani never really gave it a second thought at how often he mentioned her name. Imani was always polite, sometimes even making small talk whenever Erica answered the phone at the store. But as Imani thought of the voice on the other end of the video game earlier, she realized it was Erica’s.

Imani didn’t give the guys a chance to say anything, or clear anything up. She rushed out of the store at full speed.

Erica was a pretty girl. She was tall, slender, with brown skin and long hair. She had a young innocence about herself. She was still standing on the passenger side of the car looking down as Imani began to approach. Imani stopped dead in her tracks a few feet away and observed them both. She couldn’t believe her eyes.

Erica held her phone and said to Brandon, “Maybe I should just Google it?” Brandon never looked up, as he responded, “No, I can do it.” Brandon was on his knees, and in front of him sat a spare tire, an oily rag, and a wheel lock. Beads of sweat raced down his forehead as he held the jack in his hands, unsure of what to do with it.

Imani's emotions began to run wild. Seeing Brandon attempting to help this young woman hurt her down to the core. Although Brandon was clueless about how to change a tire, the fact that he put forth the effort, is what cut her the most.

She realized at that moment. *"A man can change for something he truly wants."* Imani couldn't remember the last time Brandon had even attempted to make an effort for her.

"Brandon!" Imani screamed in inflammatory anger. Erica and Brandon were both startled. "Oh, so now you know how to fix shit!" Imani yelled to the top of her lungs.

She began to approach the two. Erica, who was about the same weight as Imani, was visibly frightened. She quickly ran and stood behind Brandon, in which his arms suddenly became bat wings, to protect her. "Imani, don't come to my job with this mess," Brandon shouted.

Imani was all torn up. Her heart felt like it had just been ripped to shreds. Deep down inside she knew, whatever she thought she had with Brandon, was now over for good. There would be no coming back from this. But she had no plans of going away quietly.

Her eyes suddenly turned small and sinister, as her insides burned in agonizing pain.

"Oh, so this is why you changed the locks?" Imani yelled. "So, are you going to move her in next?" Imani yelled again.

Suddenly there was an audience. A few people were frozen still at their cars, a couple of teenagers slowed their pace, and a mother grabbed her small child's hand to break away from the chaos that she was sure would follow.

Brandon responded in defense mode, "This is my place of employment. You shouldn't be here. I thought this was settled when you packed your things and left. That's why I changed the locks."

Imani was seething mad. She searched for words, but she drew a blank. Brandon opened his mouth attempting to speak, but before a sound would come out, Imani took off running in the direction of their vehicles. She opened the door to her Jeep, and that's when she spotted the wine bottle. Imani grabbed the bottle just as Brandon ran in her direction with Erica following closely behind. They both were being sure to keep a safe distance away from Imani.

"Imani, this is not you. Please don't be stupid. Just let it go." Brandon pleaded.

Imani blocked him out as she proceeded to wrap her hand, tightly around the neck of the bottle. Brandon immediately threw his hands up, and backed away, fearing she may swing. In a total rage, and nearly out of breath, Imani stomped toward Brandon's car, stopping directly in front of his windshield. She lifted her right hand, and waved the bottle while yelling, "Since you like to fix shit, let me see you fix this." She then hurled the bottle at the windshield. It shattered. Imani heard “Oooh’s” and “Ahhhs” throughout the parking lot. She was in a zone. She was not herself.

Brandon yelled, “You’re goddamn nuts.” Imani stood there, with blood streaming down her hand, ready for war.

Suddenly the male and female officers, who’d just left the coffee shop, ran up to see what the commotion was all about. They noticed the blood on Imani’s hand and witnessed Brandon screaming, and immediately assumed he was the perpetrator.

The officers began to question. Brandon was so angry that he could hardly speak. He stuttered over his words, trying to explain himself.

Imani stood there looking almost possessed while viciously staring at Erica. Her eyes were wide and cold, her lips firmly pressed together, her head tilted, and her hands balled into tight fists.

Erica suddenly got a burst of courage in front of the officers and began pointing at Imani. Everything went awry from there. Imani blocked everyone out, and quickly leaped between the officers, and took a swing at the young girl. The female officer had rapid reflexes and managed to swoop Imani up before she could fully complete the blow. Imani’s baseball cap blew across the parking lot, just as she was up in the air, kicking, and screaming, all types of obscenities.

The officer said, "Ma'am you can't do that. It's called aggravated assault." Imani heard nothing. She continued to wiggle and squirm in an attempt to break free. "The officer strengthened her grip on Imani. "Calm down" She ordered. That didn't seem to register either. Suddenly the officer shouted, "Ma'am, you're resisting arrest!" The officer reached for her handcuffs and slapped them on both of Imani's wrists.

The word arrest, and feeling the heavy metal around her wrists brought Imani back to reality. She exhaled, and her body went limp. Imani bowed her head, closed her eyes, and resigned to defeat.

The officer said, "Ma'am you're under arrest for disorderly conduct, destruction of property over two hundred dollars, simple assault..." Imani didn't hear all the other charges. She just listened as the officer started to read her, her Miranda rights while walking her over to the police car. The officer opened the door, threw her in the back seat, and slammed the door shut.

Imani was scared stiff. *"What in the hell just happened?"* She asked herself.

Imani looked around, as she'd never seen the inside of a police car before. Everything in the car was black. The back seat looked like an empty shell as there was no access to windows or doors and a caged partition separated Imani from the officers. She felt numb and confused. Imani had reached one of the lowest points in her entire life.

She was flooded with emotions, as she'd never met the psychotic woman she'd recently become. She had no idea that side of her even existed. Imani had watched several Cop shows on TV and heard people plead "*temporary insanity*" all the time. She never fully understood what that meant, until a few minutes ago. Everything she'd stood for, and everything she'd been taught, was briefly voided. Her mind went blank, and the only thing she saw was her target, Erica. What a costly mistake.

Imani sat there and whimpered. She wasn't raised like that. She thought of her children. Would she be labeled unfit and lose them because of her actions? She thought of how hurt her parents would be, knowing she was going to jail. She wished that she could take it all back and start the day all over.

The female officer, who looked old enough to be her mother, stepped inside the police vehicle. "Young lady I need your name and birthdate."

"Imani McNair born April 28, 1995." She answered in a low and feeble tone.

The officer huffed, expressing her frustration as she asked the question again only louder. "Excuse me, I can't hear you. I need you to speak with that same fire you spoke with a few moments ago." The officer said in a stern, and chilling voice.

"Imani McNair born April 28, 1995." She repeated, speaking much louder than before.

Imani was humiliated and couldn't help but to revisit the past twelve hours of her life.

It started with an argument with Brandon about his love for the video game, and her putting the kids in daycare, and how she was growing tired of his ways.

Life was so strange she thought... *"This morning she contemplated how to break away. Now she found herself fighting, and trying to make him stay."*

Imani's police record came back clean. The officer glared at Imani as she stepped outside of the vehicle and joined the other officer.

Imani stared out the window and focused on Brandon. Her mood became downcast as Erica stood next to him rubbing the small of his back. *"How long had they been together? How could she had not seen the signs?"* She questioned herself.

Brandon was beside himself with anger and frustration. His eyes were bugged; his face was twisted and contorted, with his knees slightly bent as he pointed at his vehicle, surveying the damage with the officers. Her stomach became sour with disgust. The mere sight of him made her want to throw up. Brandon looked like "*A boy, crying because someone had damaged his brand new toy."* She realized that she'd been fighting for a man who wasn't worth it at all, for his car held more value than she.

Imani solemnly stared, as the officers continued to speak with Brandon and Erica when the sound of a police siren caused her to panic. She frantically looked around when another patrol car pulled up to the scene. Her heart raced, and she began to sweat when she read the words supervisor on the police cruiser.

The supervisor doubled parked the vehicle, and two male officers joined their fellow officers. Imani's hopes of walking away from this unscathed didn't seem promising. She closed her eyes and whispered to herself, *"In the palm of his hands, he held my fate, because I lost who I was and was conquered by hate."*

Imani had to face reality; she couldn't play the victim here. She understood what she had done. She had no one to blame but herself. *What was she really hoping to accomplish by coming here?* She really couldn't answer that. She knew that *"violence begets violence and hate begets hate."* Nothing was empowering or strong about breaking out Brandon's car window or attacking a young girl. Imani handed Brandon, what she was seeking, and that was *power* and *control.*

This forced her to realize that cursing, screaming, and acting a damn fool doesn't always give you power; in most cases, it takes it away. She also realized that you must accept that certain doors were shut for a reason and that sometimes, real power, and strength comes from walking away. *Something she wished she had done.*

She continued to stare, as the officers conversed for several more minutes before everyone disbursed.

Brandon and Erica headed toward Game Stop, the supervisors headed toward their vehicle, and the male and female officer headed towards her.

Imani took slow, steady breaths and braced herself, as she would soon learn her fate.

The male and female officer both stepped back inside the vehicle. The male officer started the engine. They sat there in silence for a few minutes as each officer took notes. Imani was wondering what was happening, as those minutes felt more like hours.

The female officer turned to face her. Ms. McNair, you are looking at multiple serious felonies here; assault and battery, disorderly conduct, resisting arrest, destruction of property, and that's only to name a few. No man or woman is ever worth your freedom. Attorney fees, being locked up with hardcore criminals, being away from your loved ones, not to mention having a criminal record would change the trajectory of your life for a very long time. I want you to remember these words; *"Think before you blink."*

Just when Imani thought she couldn't get any lower, she was wrong. That brief statement reminded her of that. She'd never forget it. It only took as little as five minutes, for her freedom to be up for grabs.

The female officer looked at her with empathy. Her tone was becoming soft and compassionate. "Ms. McNair I don't know you, but I have a daughter that's the same age as you are. So, I'm going to tell you what

I'd tell her. You can do better than this. You seem like a decent person, and I can only hope that you take this horrible experience and learn from it."

Imani shamefully nodded her head in agreement as the officer continued to speak.

"Ms. McNair you should consider this to be your lucky day. Mr. Garrison and Ms. Lewis will not press charges at this time. My partner here, along with my supervisors, all agree that this seems to be just one big misunderstanding since no one wants to give a witness statement. So Ms. McNair unless someone comes down to the precinct and file a complaint, we are going to let this go. "

Imani blinked a few times before exhaling. She couldn't believe what she was hearing, but she didn't question. She didn't want them to take it back. "Thank you all." She said, "I've truly learned my lesson."

"Ms. McNair, I think you should thank Mr. Garrison." The female officer said with a slight grin. The officer stepped out of the vehicle, opened Imani's door and proceeded to remove the handcuffs. She noticed that Imani was still bleeding. The officer reached inside the vehicle and handed her a few bandages. "That looks like a nasty cut on your hand; you may need to have that wrapped up. Imani was so happy to be free until she felt no pain. She surveyed the cut and said, "After all that I've been through, this little cut is nothing."

The officer gave Imani a pleasant smile as she escorted her over to her Jeep. Once Imani was safely inside, the officer spoke in a low motherly tone, "Remember what I told you." Imani repeated her words. "Think before you blink. I'll never forget that for as long as I live. Thank you."

Imani started her engine and looked straight ahead. She and Brandon were officially over, and she'd be lying if she said that it didn't hurt like hell. But she had to push forward and move on with her life. She was left with no other choice.

ൃ

It didn't matter whether she turned her Jeep to the right or the left, they both would lead to the unknown since she had no official place to call home. Of course, she could have gone to her parents, but to her, that wasn't even an option. She wanted to move forward and to go back to her parents was a giant step backward. That house was not big enough for Imani and Peter McNair. She had approximately two weeks to secure a home for her boys and herself. Time was of the essence, and she didn't have a minute to waste.

Imani decided to make a right turn on the main road, headed in the direction of LaShawn's apartment.

Imani was so grateful for her best friend; she made "adulting" look easy.

Imani witnessed how her friend started working at a hair salon right after graduation and had saved up enough money to move into a two-bedroom apartment one year later. When LaShawn turned twenty-one, she went to Bartending School, and now she's making a ton of money on the weekends at Sanchez's Bar and grill.

Everyone in their old neighborhood believed that LaShawn would be the first to become pregnant, but she proved them all wrong. She said she didn't want any kids, and she took the necessary steps to make sure that it didn't happen. The people in the neighborhood were shocked to find out it was Imani McNair who had become pregnant first.

Imani pulled into the complex and was greeted by a young man polishing his car rims while playing loud rap music. No one could possibly understand the lyrics, because it was full of bass. There were also two young mothers sitting on their balconies watching their children play outside without any shoes on and she also noticed a couple of older guys sitting at a picnic table playing dominos.

Imani hurriedly parked her car and slammed her door. She held her head down as she quickly ran up to LaShawn's apartment building.

"Damn baby slow down?" She heard one of the men yell followed by laughter.

Imani ignored the men. She rang the buzzer frantically as an indicator of it being an emergency. After several seconds, LaShawn yelled through the intercom, "It better be a fire."

"No LaShawn, it's not a fire, it's me," Imani responded. There was a short pause.

"It's just after noon; I thought we agreed on four o'clock?" LaShawn said with confusion.

"Can you please just let me in; I need to talk." Imani pleaded.

Within seconds, Imani was running up the flight of stairs to LaShawn's third-floor apartment. LaShawn stood in the doorway looking glamorous. She wore short shorts, a fitted tank top, that accented her flat stomach, silver flip-flops, with perfect hot pink toenail polish. Her long hair was swooped to one side, falling over her left shoulder, and she wore rhinestone hoop earrings with the matching bangles.

Imani dashed into LaShawn's arms the moment she saw her and burst into tears. LaShawn wrapped her arms around her, never uttering a word. LaShawn caught sight of the now bloody bandage, which Imani had wrapped around her hand. "Oh, my goodness, what happened?" LaShawn asked in a concerned voice.

Imani glanced down at the bandage with tears streaming down her face, "It's not as bad as it looks." Imani thought that she had control of her emotions, but she was wrong.

LaShawn held her friend tight, as she ushered her over to the kitchen sink. She ran Imani's hand under the water and wrapped it in paper towel while applying pressure. She patted Imani's back while whispering, "Whenever you're ready to talk, I'm here to listen."

After a few minutes, Imani pulled herself together. "Can you please hand me some tissue? I believe this is the last of them." Imani blew her nose completely, and let out a deep sigh before she was finally able to speak.

"Well, LaShawn I finally took your advice." LaShawn wore a look of confusion. She froze her neck, squinted her eyes, and pursed her lips together.

"And what advice might that be my friend?"

Imani wiped her eyes, cleared her throat, and lied. "I left Brandon. I couldn't take it anymore. I've had enough."

LaShawn gasped at Imani's words. Her mouth flew open, as she stared at her in total disbelief. Imani hated to lie to her friend, but she was too embarrassed, to tell the truth.

After a few seconds of silence, LaShawn harshly blurted, "Oh hell no! You're not going to blame this one on me. I never told you to leave Brandon. I said, have fun, live a little, make him think, but I never said to leave. Besides, I don't even have a man, so you have no business taking advice from a woman who doesn't have a relationship."

Imani began to ball her face up as if she were getting ready to cry again. She thought her friend would be happy. She never anticipated that type of response.

LaShawn sensed that the tears were soon coming, so she softened her tone. “Imani, you just said that you got the last of the tears out. I wasn’t trying to sound mean; it’s just that you caught me off guard with that one. I don’t want to be responsible, for anyone walking away from their man, because I’ve clearly never had a steady relationship like that.”

Moments later, a medium build, light skinned, male, stepped from the bathroom wearing basketball shorts, with no shirt, holding a tube of toothpaste. Imani recognized him from the bar, but she never knew his name.

“Hey, LaShawn!” He hollered in an exasperated tone. “How come I can never find my toothbrush whenever I come over here?”

LaShawn looked embarrassed that she was busted. She responded with more attitude than him. “Because you don’t live here, that’s why. Besides, don’t you see that I have company?”

He shook his head and said, “Whatever man!” and disappeared back inside the bathroom.

Imani began to head toward the door. She shook uncontrollably. “I’m sorry for popping in on you. I didn’t know you had company.”

“Oh don’t worry about him. He’s no one. I shouldn’t have taken his call since he hardly ever takes mine.”

LaShawn replied as she escorted Imani over to the couch. "Imani, I want what's best for you. I always have. But you have small children, and a few semesters of school left. I really don't think you're in the position to leave. I mean, at least wait until you're finished with school."

As gentle as LaShawn put those words, Imani still didn't quite comprehend. She viewed it as if she was being chastised.

She began to ball her face up again. In a panic, LaShawn said "Ok, Ok, Ok, please don't cry. I hate it when you cry. You're going to make me cry. Ok, now, where are the children?"

Imani began to relax. "Up North for two weeks with Brandon's parents."

LaShawn breathed a sigh of relief. "Ok, now do you have a plan?"

Imani looked at her friend and said, "Not really. That's why I'm here. I have two weeks to find a full-time job and a place to stay for my children and me. My schooling will have to wait."

LaShawn said, "What about your parents' house? You know they would welcome you back with open arms."

"No!" Imani said adamantly. "I can't go back there. I won't go back there. That house is not big enough for my father and me. I am a grown woman, not a child and I can make it on my own."

"Ok, well calm down," LaShawn said. "Now on to my next question; do you have any money? You can't do anything without money "*Ms. Grown Woman*." LaShawn said with a bit of sarcasm in her voice.

Imani opened her purse. "I have a few hundred dollars and a check from Mrs. Garrison, that I didn't have a chance look at."

"Well, I can talk to my cousin who manages this building. I know that she has a vacant two-bedroom unit," LaShawn said with optimism in her voice.

Imani paused and pursed her lips together. "I have to think about the kids."

LaShawn received the message. She took no offense. In her eyes, Imani had certain expectations. She was raised with both of her parents, in a stable, working-class home. Imani then moved from her parents' modest home, into what LaShawn considered to be a palace. She felt that her apartment complex was beneath Imani's standards.

LaShawn retracted the last statement, "I mean, I'm sure I can help you find somewhere that would be a lot more suitable for the kids."

"Thank you." Imani said as she picked up her purse and retrieved the check from her wallet. She opened it up. Her eyes became huge with her mouth agape, as she held the check with two hands.

"Why are you looking like you've never seen a check before?" LaShawn teased. "Do you want to tell me how much it is?"

Imani felt a little melancholy as she handed LaShawn the check.

"Twenty-five hundred dollars," LaShawn screamed. "Girl you crazy as hell. There's no need to look sad. You better find a way to make that relationship work, there are kids involved." She said with optimism in her voice. "Imani, I'll be right back. Let me go back here and see what type of mommy and daddy De'Andre has." LaShawn said facetiously.

Imani continued to stare at the check. Where LaShawn viewed it as a bonus, Imani did not. She knew it was far from a bonus and more of a severance package. Imani wished that she had the strength and courage to give it back. She wished that she didn't need the money because she'd love to rip the check in half and tell his mother to shove it. Her eyes became teary as she looked around at LaShawn's cozy apartment. It was freshly painted cream, with blinds to match. Beautiful African-American art lined the walls. She had a tan colored leather sectional, accented with burgundy and brown pillows, with a matching burgundy and tan rug. She had real flowers, scented candles, and beautiful picture frames throughout her apartment. The kitchen was small, but even that was decorated. She had a long tan counter with two burgundy bar stools, tan and burgundy place settings and a wine rack tucked in the corner.

LaShawn's apartment made you feel welcome and right at home. What Imani admired the most, was that it was hers. LaShawn did it all by herself, and no one could just up and tell her to leave. LaShawn's apartment was a far cry from which she came. When she lived with her mother and grandmother, Imani was never welcomed upstairs in their house, because it was full of clutter. LaShawn would always meet everyone at the back of the house, and they would go down a flight of stairs and into the basement. LaShawn had partitioned off part of the basement with sheets. That's where she did hair. But behind those sheets, you could see that the house was filled with boxes, stacks of papers and other miscellaneous items. LaShawn' claimed her mother and grandmother loved to collect things, and that they never threw anything out. But everyone loved LaShawn. They'd sit there in that cluttered house, amongst all that stuff and have their hair done, pretending as if they didn't see it. LaShawn had always been embarrassed by her upbringing, and the minute she was able to get out on her own, she did just that.

LaShawn reappeared from the back, with her company. Imani was able to get a good look at him. He was a very handsome guy, who looked to be about five or six years older than them both.

She introduced him. “De’Andre this is my girl, Imani. Imani, this is my friend De’Andre.” They both said hello and smiled at each other, as LaShawn walked him to the door.

Before leaving, he reached into his pocket and handed her a few bills. “I’m leaving out of town on business for a few days, and I want to take you out as soon as I return. LaShawn looked down at the bills and said, “Thanks, but I have to check my calendar.” He let out a friendly laugh, reached inside his pocket, and pulled out a few more bills. “Hopefully this will buy me a slot.”

LaShawn took the bills and shoved them right back in his hand. “De’Andre I make my own money. I can’t be bought.” She gave him a huge smile and said, “Call me when you’re back in town.” He left out the door shaking his head saying, “You sure are different.”

When LaShawn closed the door, Imani was filled with total admiration. Imani loved the control and power that came along with having your own. She was also confused, so she asked, “Why on Earth did you give him his money back?”

LaShawn let out a deep sigh and said, “Because that’s no longer enough. You see, In the beginning, it was easy to accept his money because we were having fun.” She half-smiled, ”friends with benefits. But now I really like him, and I’m ready to take the relationship to the next level.”

Imani looked perplexed. “I don’t understand.”

LaShawn explained, “De’Andre and I met eight months ago at the bar, and the attraction was instant. The chemistry between us both is like nothing I’ve ever experienced before.”

Imani had to stop her right there. “Well how come I’ve never heard about him before today?”

LaShawn sighed. “Because it’s complicated. De’Andre is a truck driver who’s over the road a lot, and the time just isn’t there. Therefore, I keep my expectations to a minimum. His job takes precedence over everything. Money means everything to him, whereas living and exploring life means everything to me. He’s trying desperately to hold on to us both, but I’m afraid it’s not working out. Him throwing money at me is his way of trying to keep me still. He believes that by giving me money, it will hold him a seat at the table; or in his case, a slot in the toothbrush holder.”

Imani and LaShawn both let out a laugh.

“Wow. That’s deep! Have you ever told him how you feel?” Imani asked.

“He knows. But I would never want to make a man choose between his job and me. I also don’t want any man to think he can buy my loyalty or a commitment. He must earn it. If he wants a slot in that toothbrush holder, he must earn that as well. I do still enjoy his company, so that’s why I let him hang around. However, it’s really getting old. But don’t worry, when I’m tired, he’ll know. As far as his money goes, I can make my own." LaShawn said while cutting her eyes and snapping her fingers. "Now come on, let's go and get you all dolled up. Maybe that will help make you feel better." She said to Imani.

An hour later, LaShawn had Imani looking like a million bucks. She'd washed and pressed her hair, and put it up in a neat bun. LaShawn polished her nails, waxed her eyebrows, and gave her a soft makeover. She handed Imani the mirror. "You look so beautiful."

Imani looked at herself in the mirror and thought she did look pretty. She only wished that she could make the inside, feel just as good as the outside.

LaShawn snapped her fingers once more, "Step into my studio so that I can find you something to wear. Once I'm done, I want you to stroll up to Brandon's job, and show him what he's missing."

Imani lowered the mirror and stared at her best friend with sadden eyes and spoke in an earnest voice, "Brandon and I are over. I'm not doing this for him; I'm doing this for me. He had his chance, and he blew it. He doesn't even deserve to see me."

LaShawn wore a meek expression and slightly bowed her head. "I understand my friend."

LaShawn escorted Imani over to her spare bedroom where she had a sign with flashing lights that read, "The Bling Studio."

LaShawn opened the door to what looked like a celebrity dressing room. There was a plush love seat, a table with a sewing machine, an ironing board and a hot glue gun. She had all of her craft materials neatly assembled on the table. There were T-shirts, denim jackets and jeans, belt buckles, and hats. Imani even noticed a panty and bra set all ready to be blinged out. Above the table was a message board with photos of local rappers, singers, and musicians, all wearing bling designs by LaShawn.

The girl was super-talented. Once she saw Imani's eyes light up, she said, "Do you like my room? I just finished putting it together a few weeks ago."

Imani said, "Girl you really have it going on. How come you won't start your own business? This room is beautiful. I think you need more space though because it's a little cramped in here with all of this stuff."

"Hey, cut it out, Imani. You know that's in my DNA. I come from, a family of hoarders." LaShawn laughed. "But unlike my mom and grandmother, I know where everything is, and I use all my stuff. I love doing this work, and these artists take care of me, but since I don't have a business license or a tax ID number, I can only take donations. I'm afraid of the IRS. That's why I've been pressuring my best friend *'Imani McNair'* about finishing school and getting that business degree so that she can help set me up. I can make the stuff. It's just that I have no idea on how to run a legitimate business."

Imani looked at her and said, "Well you have to hold on a little while longer. School is on the back burner for now."

The two stepped over boxes, and shoes, and made it over to her closet. They searched amongst all of her beautiful things until they found the perfect sundress and sandals for Imani.

"Some man is going to be so lucky to have you," LaShawn said while offering her friend a hug.

LaShawn started gathering up her things. "Well girlfriend, I have to leave you. I have a few customers to do this afternoon at the salon, and then it's off to the mall for a little shopping and a full body massage. I'll be at Sanchez's this evening."

LaShawn reached inside a drawer and handed Imani a spare key. "Make yourself at home. I hope you don't mind sleeping on this couch in the studio. It's all I have. I promise the first thing tomorrow morning; I'll help you find a place."

Imani was grateful. "I can manage it from here. You've been a great help, and I promise, you won't even know I'm here."

As LaShawn stepped out the door, Imani realized how much she admired her friend. The fact that she had nothing standing in her way, and had total control over her life, made Imani second-guess her poor decision-making. Imani loved her kids with all her heart, but if she could do it all over again, she believed she would have waited.

ↅ

Finding an apartment was much more complicated than Imani had realized. She scoured the apartment guide booklets, and nothing seemed to be within her budget. The better apartments that were suitable to her taste were priced at one thousand dollars a month and up. She soon understood why LaShawn was comfortable living where she was.

Imani drove around and searched for hours until she finally found an apartment that was reasonably priced. It was located in a relatively nice area of the city and was accessible to several expressways. The sign caught her eye. "Eight hundred and fifty dollars Move-in Special." She liked the price more than anything. She smiled and said to herself; things seem to be looking up after-all.

Imani applied more lip-gloss, straightened out her dress, and walked tall inside the rental office. Since this would be her first major accomplishment on her own, she wanted to make a great impression.

A tall, dark, handsome, middle-aged African American gentleman greeted her at the door with a smile.

He extended his hand and gave her a firm handshake. She told him what she was looking for, and he was happy to assist. He escorted Imani down the hall into a two-bedroom unit. "This is the one that's on special, it's called the Classic, and it's the last one left, so you have to act fast," he said.

When he said that she had to act fast, Imani began to feel overwhelmed. She was positive that she wanted to move; she just didn't want to be rushed into a decision on the spot.

When she stepped into the unit, she was slightly disappointed as she understood why it was called the Classic. Although it was clean, it was small and hadn't been updated. The carpet was dark brown, the cabinets were dark brown, the walls were beige, and the floors and countertops were an off-white color. It wasn't fancy at all.

She thought of what her father would say. "No matter how bad things may seem, always try to find some good in every situation."

She then began to imagine what it would look like once she added furniture, some paintings, and accessories. It'll be just fine she thought to herself. At least it will be my own, and no one can tell me to leave. Most importantly, the boys would have their own space.

Imani smiled as she turned to the gentleman and said, "I'll take it."

He returned the smile and said, "Great! So in order to start the process, I'll need fifty dollars for the non-refundable application fee, a valid driver's license, current check stubs, bank statements, references, and you will also need first month's rent, along with the security deposits and..."

"Huhhhh!" was all Imani could say as he continued to rattle off the list of things she needed. Her heart felt as if it was going to leap right out of her chest. She didn't have half those things.

Imani responded, "Can you just write down the list of things that I need so that I can bring them back to you in a couple of days?"

He smiled and kindly gave her a brochure. "I hope to see you soon because, without a deposit, I can't guarantee that this unit will be available when you come back.

Imani grabbed the brochure and said, "I'll take my chances." As she exited the apartment, a young, enthusiastic couple stepped in, "We're here to take a look at the apartment that's on special."

Imani ran to her Jeep and snatched the door open. She sat there for a few seconds before she pounded both fists on the steering wheel. "Damn!" She yelled. "I can't do this on my own. This is hard."

The vibration of her cell phone startled her. She rummaged through her purse and retrieved it. She had missed the call. In fact, she'd missed several calls. They all were from her parents' home. The phone rang again. She wanted to hit ignore, but she knew they'd keep calling.

"Hello, Mom," Imani answered. Her mother let out a deep breath. "Imani honey, your father and I are worried sick about you. We've been calling you for the past few hours. When you didn't pick up, your father called Brandon. He mentioned that you and he had some sort of an altercation and that the police were involved."

Imani was furious that Brandon had the temerity to mention what had transpired earlier to her parents. He knew it would set her father off. This now only exacerbated the disdain and bitterness that she felt for him.

She had to think fast and get her mother off the phone.

"Hello mom, there's a bad connection. You're breaking up." Imani said lying. Her mother tried repeating herself, but Imani interrupted her. "Mom, I'm fine. I'll call you back later." Before Imani would end the call, she could hear her mother pleas, "Please come home baby, we love you. Your father wants to speak with you."

"Imani!" Her father barked into the phone. Hearing the baritone sound of his voice caused her to end the call immediately. She knew nothing good would come from that phone conversation. He would only demand that she came back home right away.

A few seconds later, her phone chimed. She let out a heavy breath before looking at the message. This time it was LaShawn.

It read: "Can you please stop by the bar and pick up the tickets from Mr. Sanchez? He has three tickets to the Rap Fest this evening at the Fillmore Detroit."

"Sure," Imani responded.

LaShawn replied, "Oh, I forgot to mention, you're going along with my girl Candy and me. No excuses! I already told Mr. Sanchez we wouldn't be in tonight."

Imani tried to think of a reason not to go, but she couldn't come up with a legitimate one since LaShawn knew her circumstances.

LaShawn sent a final text, "You're not wearing that sundress either. I already have your clothes picked out. Let the party begin!!!"

Oh boy, this should be interesting, Imani thought to herself since rap music was her least favorite genre.

ଔ

The time was four o'clock in the afternoon when she pulled up to Sanchez's Bar and Grill. Mr. Sanchez's van, along with two other cars were in the parking lot. Imani stepped inside the bar and greeted the two older gentlemen who were sitting at the bar, sipping beer and listening to the blues on the sound system. Mr. Sanchez stood behind the bar taking inventory.

Imani sat down and called his name. "Hey Mr. Sanchez, can I get a glass of red wine please?"

Mr. Sanchez slowly turned around and noticed what she was wearing. It was the first thing that caught his eye. The beautiful yellow dress matched her beautiful bright smile. *What a difference a day makes*, he thought.

"Imani, what a pleasure it is to see you," he said offering her a big wide smile. "That dress looks lovely on you. You just may have me to re-think the dress code around here."

"Well, I don't think the girls would be too fond of that," Imani said with a laugh.

Mr. Sanchez poured Imani a glass of red wine and handed her the tickets to the concert.

"I have no idea who these folks are, but LaShawn sure does." Mr. Sanchez said with a laugh. "One of my wine vendors dropped them off today. I hope you guys have a great time, and please be safe."

Imani looked at Mr. Sanchez and said with very little enthusiasm, "I'll try." She then gulped down the wine and slapped seven dollars on the counter.

He gave her one last reassuring smile and said, "Make the best of it."

ഗ

Imani pulled into the apartment complex, and it was busy as usual. A young man tinkered with a motorized dirt bike, a few young boys, dribbled a basketball in the middle of the parking lot, and a couple of teenage girls wearing short summer dresses, sat provocatively at the picnic table vying for the boy's attention. *"Don't these people ever take a break?"* She said to herself.

Imani finally made it inside of the apartment. She was dead tired. Exhausted. She'd had one of the longest, most dreadful days of her life.

"She'd fought with Brandon, went home to her parents, became officially homeless, had another fight with Brandon, almost went to jail, went apartment hunting, and in a few hours she'd be on her way to a rap concert.

Imani headed straight to the studio and stepped out of the sundress, removed the boxes and t-shirts that were on the sofa and stacked them neatly in the corner. She grabbed a blanket, and a pillow and immediately fell into a deep sleep.

She had no idea how long she'd been sleeping when she heard laughing, music, and feet moving around the apartment. Imani was too exhausted to look up at the time, so she rolled over and placed the pillow over her head. Suddenly, LaShawn burst into the room yelling, laughing, while holding her cell phone. "Hey girl, get your butt up, it's six thirty in the evening! You've had enough rest. It's time for us to get this party started."

Imani rolled back over and asked LaShawn without even opening her eyes, "Do I really have to go?" LaShawn snatched the covers off her and said, "Heck yes. You're not getting out of this one. I haven't had you to myself in a long time, and your kids are out of town, so no excuses. Plus, I know you'll probably run back to Brandon, so I might as well enjoy you while I can."

Imani finally opened her eyes. When she looked at her friend, she couldn't believe how spectacular she looked. If she didn't personally know her, she would have thought she was some big pop star.

LaShawn's hair extensions were long and put into a sleek ponytail that fell to the center of her back. Her eyebrows were sculpted to perfection, the lashes were long and spiked, her eye makeup was bright, her cheeks were highlighted, and the hot pink lipstick she wore made her entire face pop. She wore a sparkling white bustier that had tiny crystals all over it; accented by ripped jean shorts, a crystal belt and she topped it off with a pair of designer cowboy boots.

Imani sat up straight and said, "Wow! Did you make that?"

LaShawn, said, "Everything except the boots. I've been saving this for a special occasion, and I believe this concert is the one." She gave Imani her phone.

"Please snap my picture." Imani snapped a few pictures, and LaShawn snapped a few selfies, and immediately uploaded it to Instagram. "Ughh," Imani thought, I hate social media. Imani was a private person. She believed that social media was too intrusive, so she didn't engage in it.

"Now go freshen up, I have something for you to wear as well," LaShawn said full of energy.

When Imani emerged from the bathroom, she saw the items of clothing that LaShawn had selected for her. There was a pair of ripped blue jeans, a white ribbed tank top, and a pair of white sandals covered in crystals. Imani was pleased when she saw what she would be wearing because she didn't have even half the confidence of LaShawn.

Imani stepped out of the room fully dressed. She thought she looked great, but from the bleak expression on LaShawn's face, it didn't meet her approval rating. "Come back into the bathroom. I need to do your face." LaShawn demanded.

Imani shook her head thinking... *I knew this was too simple.*

When LaShawn was done, Imani examined herself in the mirror and was amazed by her own transformation. She looked like a star, but a milder version of her friend. LaShawn applied lashes, blended her eyeshadow to perfection, as well as her cheeks, and she topped it off with light pink, gloss on her lips.

"You like?" LaShawn asked wearing a big smile.

"Yes," Imani said. "Although I don't think I could do this every day. These lashes feel weird." They both laughed. "

You'll be fine," LaShawn said as she handed Imani a pair of custom, stoned, hoop earrings, with a jean jacket covered in Swarovski crystals on the pockets, around the collar, and the sleeves.

Imani, laughed as she put the jacket on, "I knew my outfit was too simple." She said teasing her friend. LaShawn gave her a wink.

"Here, take some of my business cards, and put them in your pockets. This is how I attract new customers." LaShawn said.

As they were dressed and ready to go, the doorbell rang. LaShawn answered, and her friend Candy yelled into the intercom, "Heeeeeeey, it's me." LaShawn immediately buzzed her up. Candy looked just as fabulous as Imani and LaShawn. She wore a baseball cap, a jean jacket, and short shorts, all emblazoned in Swarovski crystals. LaShawn hugged both girls and snapped a selfie in the process. Imani was annoyed. Her eyes were half closed, but LaShawn didn't care, she posted the picture anyway. "Ughhh" "I hate social media," Imani said to herself.

Lashawn said, "Hey, let's toast up before we go."

"You two can drink up. I already had a glass of wine at the bar earlier. LaShawn we'll take your car, and I'll be the designated driver." Imani said.

LaShawn looked at Imani with skepticism, and said, "Alright. But I'm going to need you to loosen up and enjoy yourself. We don't need a mother hen tonight." She joked.

As they began to approach the "Fillmore Detroit" the traffic on Woodward Avenue became congested. Everyone was out in search of a good time. The Detroit Tigers were playing at Comerica Park, people were blasting rap music in their cars, there was dancing in front of the building, along with ticket scalpers trying to get those last-minute sales.

Imani handed the keys to the valet, and before she could get her nerves and bearings in check, she'd noticed that LaShawn and Candy were many steps ahead of her. They strutted through the crowds of people like they owned the place. They were in their element.

Imani tried, but she couldn't manage to muster up the enthusiasm and excitement as those two, so she ambled behind praying that she'd make it through the evening. LaShawn slowed her pace, and turned to Imani and said, "Come on Grandma, let's hurry up and make it into the building."

As Imani began to catch up, LaShawn suddenly became bombarded by several young ladies, all asking, "Who made those outfits?" LaShawn began handing out her business cards. She then yelled at the crowd, "follow me on Twitter, hashtag bling by LaShawn."

Imani smiled as she watched her friend work. Everyone has some sort of unique skill, gift, or talent; and creativity was LaShawn's. She deserved to be in Hollywood designing clothes for the stars because she definitely had what it took.

Once they made it inside the venue, LaShawn and Candy headed straight for the bar. They ordered wine while Imani opted for a coke. LaShawn huffed, and cut her eyes at Imani. As LaShawn proceeded to hand over the cash for the drinks, a deep males voice called from behind, "Ladies, let me pay for those." All three ladies immediately turned around. Imani and LaShawn's eyes bulged, with excitement as the tall, chivalrous man who seemed so out of place marched his way to the front of the line. He ordered another glass of wine, and handed the server a crisp fifty-dollar bill. He gave the server a sharp nod of the head and said, "Keep the change."

Imani was excited, she hadn't seen Kevin Black since they'd went to the prom several years prior. She couldn't help but notice how he looked and sounded like a more self-assured version of his younger self. Kevin lost both his parents at an early age, so he was known for being bitter, reclusive, and socially awkward. But as Imani observed him in the flesh, there were no traces of any of that. The bitterness had been exchanged for strength, his upright posture said confidence, and his proper, concise, English was unapologetic. The dress slacks, button-down shirt, and wireframe glasses sent a message to the crowd that said he was a man who didn't follow trends. He was comfortable in his own skin.

"Kevin, it's so great to see you." Imani and LaShawn both said with girlish smiles.

Kevin offered a broad smile as he leaned forward to embrace both of the women. "It's so great to see you two as well." He replied. "LaShawn, I spotted you from the door. Even as a young girl, you always knew how to stop a crowd." He turned toward Imani. "Imani, you sure have changed throughout the years, but you look fantastic as well." He looked over at Candy and said, "I don't believe we've ever met, but you look lovely also."

Imani couldn't resist. "Well Kevin, you still look like the smart, courteous, intellectual, man that I remember. I would have never in a million years guessed that I'd run into you at a rap concert."

Kevin laughed. "Well since the law firm I work for represents one of the artists, I figured I'd return the support. The free tickets were a great incentive as well." He laughed.

Kevin looked down at his watch. "Listen, ladies; I don't want to hold you up. Enjoy the concert, the wine, and please don't drink and drive." He offered one last embrace, and they all headed in the same direction towards their seats.

Once the ladies were settled into their third-row seats, the lights blinked a few times. The crowd roared. The show was about to begin. Imani felt so uncomfortable amongst the throngs of people. She looked over at LaShawn and Candy. Those two were having the time of their lives. They had both hands raised in the air, and they screamed "Hooooo Oooo," as the announcer introduced the first rapper. Imani had no idea who the rapper was, or what he sang; she just smiled, and threw her hands up, to keep from hearing LaShawn's mouth. She secretly wished that she could have sat with Kevin.

The concert went on for what seemed like forever. LaShawn and Candy never lost their energy. Imani just wanted it to end. It didn't sound like music to her, because she couldn't understand a word they were saying. The lyrics sounded muffled, highlighted by booming bass.

She thought of what her father told her when she moved in with Brandon at such a young age. *"Honey, you're so young. You should be out having fun, doing teenage stuff, there's plenty of time for marriage."* She thought about how wrong he was. If this were his idea of having fun, she'd have to pass. She realized that she was a young woman born with an old soul and she was ok with that. You could give her the music she grew up listening to with her father, Aretha Franklin,

Anita Baker, Smokey Robinson, Earth Wind and Fire or anything Motown and she'd be happy.

It was close to the last act when Imani noticed the security guard whispering something to LaShawn, whose eyes were all aglow. He handed her an envelope. LaShawn smiled as she whispered something back. Imani had no idea what the exchange was all about; she just wanted to get the heck out of that theater.

After the final act, there was a thunderous applause as the lights came on. Imani's eyes panned the building staring at all the happy people. It seemed as if everyone had a great time except for her. Then suddenly she looked three rows ahead, and that's when she saw her. It was Erica, Brandon's girlfriend. Erica was standing next to the stage surrounded by a group of young girls, yelling, screaming, and frantically waving their hands. They looked like young groupies attempting to get an autograph from the rapper who had just performed. Imani sat there in disbelief. *"He cheated on me for that slut?"* She said to herself.

Imani surveyed the area again when her eyes suddenly landed on Brandon. They briefly locked eyes before she quickly looked away. Her heart thumped, as he, seemed just as out of place as she. But the embarrassment in his eyes spoke volumes, as his young paramour and her girls stood there like rap star groupies.

Imani had a sinking feeling in her stomach. Seeing Brandon and Erica out together hurt her down to the core. But, before Imani would have the chance to sulk, it seemed as though the universe had sensed her pain, and had stepped in to offer her relief. At that very moment, Kevin Black walked up the aisle amongst a crowd of people.

"Kevin," Imani called out to him in a frenzied voice. Kevin leaned in, and without thinking, Imani pulled him close to her. She wrapped her arms tightly around his neck, closed her eyes, and hung there like a loose neck-tie. She wanted Brandon to see her; she wanted him to know that she was not sitting at home feeling sorry for herself. Imani felt awful for using Kevin that way, but he was the only comfort she could find. LaShawn and Candy were so wrapped up into the show until they paid her no mind.

Imani could feel Kevin start to pull away. She opened her eyes as she released herself from the embrace. Kevin wore a look of confusion on his face as he cupped his hands over his mouth. That's when Imani noticed he was wearing a wedding band. Kevin quickly reached out to the young woman who was standing close by. She also wore a wedding ring.

Imani felt as though she'd die right there on the spot. She'd just made a complete fool of herself. But, she had to find a way to clean it up. She couldn't possibly leave Kevin standing there without rectifying things. He was a great person who didn't deserve to be used as a pawn.

"Kevin! Oh my God, it's so great to see you." Imani went on with a wide plastered smile. "You were my childhood best friend. It's been a long time since we've last seen each other." Imani continued to smile as she pointed to the woman standing next to him. "My parent's told me you'd gotten married. This must be your lovely wife?" Imani wasn't sure if he'd mentioned to his wife about running into her at the bar earlier, but it was the best she could offer under the circumstances. She hoped that she'd sounded convincing and not made things worse.

Kevin let out a soft breath of relief and remained calm as he played along with Imani's game. "Imani McNair, it's so great to see you as well. Yes, this is my beautiful wife, Tonya," He said as he looked at his wife adoringly. "Tonya this is Imani, we've known each other since we were kids. Our families are neighbors." Kevin looked down at his watch before looking back up at Imani with a sly sarcastic smile. "And it certainly has been a minute since we've last seen each other." Imani chuckled to herself at his inside joke. Kevin had always been an intellectual and the last she'd heard he was studying law. So him manipulating the facts so quickly didn't surprise her one bit. Imani took it all in stride because it seems as though she'd asked for it.

Imani looked at Tonya and offered her a friendly smile as she shook her hand. "Well, Tonya, it's so nice to meet you. You and Kevin seem like a wonderful couple, and I wish you both many years of happiness."

Tonya returned the smile as she looked up at her husband. Kevin reached down and planted a kiss on her lips. Tonya then said, “Thank-you, I appreciate your kind words.”

As Kevin and Tonya walked away holding hands, Imani was filled with envy. Her mood quickly became somber. Growing up she had never found Kevin to be desirable; she thought he was weird. But as she stood there and looked at the finished product, she realized that she was either too young, too immature or simply too myopic to notice what a great human being he always was. “*Tonya is one lucky lady*.” Imani whispered to herself.

After Imani managed to pick her face up off the floor, she looked around for LaShawn and Candy. *She’d endured enough pain for one evening.*

LaShawn and Candy stood there taking selfies when LaShawn noticed that Imani had stepped away. LaShawn called out to her, “Imani, get over here.” She demanded. ”You’re missing out on all the photos.” Imani rejoined the girls and let out a painful smile. LaShawn bear hugged Imani and Candy. “Ladies, this was one of the best concerts I’ve attended in a while.” Candy agreed.

Imani said meekly, “Yes, this was some concert.”

LaShawn said, “Oh the fun isn’t over. Look what I have.” She held up the envelope and started dancing while chanting, “Tickets to the after-party. Who hooooo!” She sang.

Imani thought she'd pass out right there in the theater. "After-party? Oh, hell no!" She said firmly. LaShawn and Candy were so excited that they paid her attitude no mind. They jumped up and down as if they'd just won the lottery.

"Yes after-party," LaShawn said again still excited. "The security guard asked to follow me on Instagram. One of the groups backstage liked our outfits. He gave me these tickets so that we can meet the artist up close and personal."

"LaShawn, I'm exhausted, and I definitely don't want to go to any after party, please take me back to your place, or I'll call an Uber. I just can't do it!" Imani said adamantly.

LaShawn looked at Imani and huffed. "Oh alright, Grandma, we'll drop you off. I will not let you spoil the rest of my evening."

Imani was happy. She didn't care what LaShawn called her, as long as she got her the heck out of there.

ଓ

Imani awoke to thumping music, the strong smell of marijuana, and loud voices. She was so tired that she had to look around to remember where she was. She grabbed her phone and looked at the time. It was three forty-five a.m. She tiredly hopped up and peeked out the bedroom door. She was flabbergasted at what she saw. *"Oh my God, this can't be happening*," she whispered to herself through tears. LaShawn had brought the after-party back to her place. It must have been at least fifteen people in her apartment. They were playing cards, drinking excessively, and smoking marijuana. Imani witnessed a couple of guys rapping while a few people chanted as LaShawn and Candy danced. *"This is unreal,"* Imani said to herself as she slammed the studio door shut. Imani found herself once again with her back against the wall, both hands cupping her eyes, as she sobbed uncontrollably. *"Why me?"* She said to herself.

Imani had to get her own. There was no way that she could live like this. She was lost now more than ever.

Imani needed: Peace, comfort, control, and a sound mind. They all went hand in hand. One couldn't properly function without the other.

When you lose your peace, you lose your comfort, when you lose your comfort, you lose control, and when you lose control, you lose your mind." And if she didn't find a place fast, she would definitely lose her mind.

The party continued until a little after five in the morning. Imani sat on the couch and counted the minutes when the music abruptly stopped.

"Ok, that's it! The party is over! I need everyone to get your things and get out. I'm sleepy." LaShawn said in an authoritative tone. Imani heard a few “Awwwws,” But LaShawn meant what she’d said, because soon after, Imani heard people moving about, bottles clanking, and the front door opening and closing.

ꕥ

The time was eight forty-five in the morning when Imani heard the alarm on her cell phone. She jumped straight up, as she had no time to waste. She had precisely thirteen days to secure a home for her boys and herself.

Imani was in and out of the bathroom in less than twenty minutes. She folded her blanket, gathered her few belongings before knocking on LaShawn’s door.

“Come in.” LaShawn faintly answered.

Imani peeked inside her room and whispered, “I’m leaving now. I appreciate you letting me stay here. I’ll be out of your hair soon.”

LaShawn’s voice was groggy as she responded, “Girl you’re fine. You can stay as long as you like. I hope we didn’t keep you up. It’s just that I had made so many connections last night that I had plenty of reasons to celebrate. The after-party just kind of spilled over to my place.”

Imani said, “Oh it’s your place. I’m just a guest. It didn’t bother me. I slept right on through it all.”

LaShawn joked, “Ok, well please hurry up and get settled because I need you to finish school. With all the orders that I took last night, I’m almost certain that I’m going to need a business manager.”

Imani smiled, “We’ll talk later.”

Chrysalis

Imani made it to Chase bank just before ten. She was angry with herself for not opening a bank account sooner. Her father helped to pay for her schooling, as well as her car insurance and Brandon's parents never made her pay any bills, so she never really felt the need to have a checking account. Today that would all change. Imani didn't want her parents to help her any longer. She was an adult, and she would act as such.

She'd left out of the bank thirty minutes later feeling proud and accomplished. A bank account was something she could check off her list. She'd put two thousand dollars into a checking account, and five hundred dollars into a savings account. She'd also received a book of starter checks and a debit card. She hated the fact that she had to use her parents' address for the checks, but she was left with no choice. She had no address of her own.

She sat in the parking lot and dialed Mrs. Garrison's phone number. She hadn't spoken to the boys since they'd left the day before and she missed them. Her heart raced as she stared at the numbers. Imani thought about the altercation she'd had with Brandon at his job and she was fearful of what Mrs. Garrison reaction would be. *Would she remain neutral, or would she choose sides?* Imani took a deep breath and braced herself as she hit send.

"Hello, Imani." Mrs. Garrison answered, in a brisk and dismissive tone.

"Hello Mrs. Garrison, how is everything?" Imani asked nervously.

"Everything is fine." She said, in the same terse voice, never bothering with any small talk. Before Imani could ask another question, the phone became silent. She could hear Mrs. Garrison yelling out to the boys that their mom was on the phone. Imani's feelings were hurt. She and Mrs. Garrison had become close throughout the years. But Imani understood. Mrs. Garrison loved her son, and that love trumped everything; including the bond that they had established with each other throughout the years. Imani had to accept the fact, "right, wrong or indifferent," Brandon was her son, and Mrs. Garrison's loyalty would always remain with her son.

Imani kept her conversation with her boys brief as she was afraid of what they might ask. Once the conversation ended, Imani had decided that she wouldn't call again. She'd see them when they returned. Her children were with their grandparents, and they were safe. If there was a problem, the Garrison's knew how to contact her. Her determination to keep moving forward was now more essential than ever. She had no time for regrets. She had to get going.

ɞ

Imani looked fixated at the wooden sign, “The McNair’s” for several seconds before she rang the bell.” Her father was at work, so she knew her mother was home alone. She’d planned it that way.

Mrs. McNair wore a look of relief when she laid eyes on her daughter. She dropped the laundry basket she was holding, and extended her arm and caressed Imani’s face. She spoke softly. “How are you doing?”

Imani gently removed her mother’s hand. “Mom, it’s ok. I’m fine.”

“Do you need me to help you with your bags?” Her mother said, assuming that she was there to stay.

Mrs. McNair’s relief quickly faded as Imani responded, “I didn’t come here to stay. I came here to let you and my dad know, that I was ok.” Imani said with a half smile.

Mrs. McNair wasn’t giving up so quickly, “Well I’d just hung up the phone with Linda Garrison, and we both agreed that it would be a good idea if you came back here to live.”

Imani paused. She became agitated. “Mom! I don’t need anyone making decisions for me, and definitely not the Garrisons. I run my own life.” She snapped.

Mrs. McNair was shocked at the tone in which Imani spoke. She’d never witnessed that side of her daughter before, so she trod lightly. She didn’t want Imani to shut her out.

“Well, Imani no one is trying to run your life. We’re both just worried about you that’s all.” Her mother said.

Imani gave a weak smile and said, “There’s nothing to worry about, I have everything under control.”

Mrs. McNair was concerned, so she asked, “Well where are you staying?” Your father believes that you are coming back home. We’ve even made your brother’s clean out the spare room.”

Imani interrupted her again. “Thanks for the invitation, but that won’t be necessary, I found a place. It’ll be ready in a few days, so I’m hanging out at LaShawn’s until I can move in.” She said firmly.

Mrs. McNair gave a surprised look. “Your own place? Where?” What about your children? What about your schooling? You only have a few days left to register, or you’ll have to sit out a semester.”

Imani took a long pause. She knew that she was going to hurt her mother’s feelings with her next statement, but she could not lie.

“Mom, my children will be fine. And I’m sorry, but I have to sit this semester out. My life is hectic right now, and I need to get it back into some sort of order. I plan to work full-time, so school will have to wait." Imani felt bad since she'd promised her parents that she'd be finished with school by the next fall. But she also remembered what her father said to her at the beginning of her relationship with Brandon, "Things Change. People change." Now sadly, her plans for school were a part of those changes. That was a promise, which she presently couldn't keep.

Mrs. McNair wore a look of disappointment as she looked Imani square in the eyes, and offered her a stern piece of sage advice. "Imani I hope you know what you're doing because this isn't only about you. You have children, and those children never asked to be here. Your needs and your children's needs should never be in conflict. It has been my experience that good things happen, to people who put their children first."

Imani nodded her head agreeing with her mother. "Yes ma'am, I understand. But mom, I need you to trust me. I got this." Imani said with confidence.

Mrs. McNair sighed and said, "I sure hope so."

"Hey, I'm starving, do you have any left-over breakfast?" Imani asked, quickly changing the subject.

Mrs. McNair said, "Sure. Just as soon as I drop this load in the washing machine, I'll fix you something."

As Mrs. McNair exited the room, the telephone rang. She yelled to Imani, "Can you answer that please?" Imani stepped over to the phone and looked at the caller ID. It read "Peter McNair." She quickly stepped away from the phone and headed out the door. She was in no mood to listen to her father. She heard her mother yell once more for her to answer the phone. It was no use. Imani was out the door, inside her Jeep, and headed on to her next destination.

☙

Imani pulled up directly next to Mr. Sanchez as he unloaded boxes from the back of his van. She lowered her window, and waved while flashing all of her teeth. "Need a hand?" She asked in the friendliest voice she could muster.

He looked over at her with admiration because she reminded him so much of his late wife when she was her age. He liked her simple beauty, her soft smile, and her kind personality; he always welcomed her presence.

"Sure." He said beaming as he waved her over. Imani exited her vehicle and began helping Mr. Sanchez unload the boxes from the van.

When they were done, Imani slid into a seat at the bar. "Red wine?" Mr. Sanchez asked, remembering what she'd ordered the last time.

"Yes," Imani replied.

Mr. Sanchez stepped from behind the bar and sat next to her. "So, tell me, Imani, what's going on with you? It has to be something because you haven't been yourself lately."

Imani had no idea, what it was about Mr. Sanchez, but he made her feel so comfortable, and she trusted him. The brief discussion she had with him the other day made her feel as though he understood her. She felt as though she could be herself.

Imani sipped her wine and started from the beginning. She told him about her love for her parents and her sheltered upbringing. Hooking up with Brandon her first semester in college, becoming pregnant shortly after, and the agreement they'd made with his parents. Imani discussed the two fights she had with Brandon, the police, and her being locked out of their home and how she had exactly thirteen days to find a full-time job and an apartment.

Mr. Sanchez looked at Imani in total disbelief and didn't say a word. It seemed as if he didn't quite know what to say. It was too much to process. Several seconds went by before he was finally able to speak.

"Wow! I'm tired, just listening to all of that. I'm so sorry that this is happening to you. That's such a heavy load for one person to carry alone." He said with empathy.

Imani looked at Mr. Sanchez and fought back the tears. "I'm ok." She then chuckled a bit. "I never realized how strong I was until my back was against the wall."

Mr. Sanchez let out a kind smile, "Yes you are strong. I'm so happy that you didn't go to jail, and that you've learned your lesson. I can't tell you how many times, I've witnessed people losing control and having to pay a heavy price because of it. That young man knew he was out of line, so I applaud him for letting it go. Hopefully, soon, you two can get past this because your children need you both."

Imani was still angry with Brandon, and the wound was too fresh. "Mr. Sanchez, It may take me years, if ever, to get over this one. I feel as though he's stolen some of the best years of my life. He didn't want to grow up. He's a child, and I am angry that he led me on. That won't easily be forgotten." She retorted.

Mr. Sanchez understood both points of view; however, he wouldn't speak bad about another man, to that man's woman. That was just a man code, and he'd always honor that code. So he switched gears and focuses on her. "Why can't you go back home with your parents and finish school?" He said. "You know that pride comes before the fall."

Imani pursed her lips, closed her eyes and slowly shook her head. "Please understand that this doesn't have anything to do with pride. I am a grown woman, and I want to make it on my own. I've been away from home for almost five years, and there's no way that I can go back to following Peter McNair's rules. He's demanding, controlling, and still sees me as his little girl."

Mr. Sanchez offered a light smile. "I understand. I have three daughters of my own, so I know how it is when women want their independence. Although my youngest daughter was never that considerate," he laughed. "She stayed with me and spent up my money until the day she married and moved to Florida a year after her mother's passing." He laughed again, "I didn't mind. I love my children, and they can have whatever they want from me. All my girls are happily married with children. They haven't been back here in a few years although I do talk to them every week.

Imani asked, "So where do they live?"

His voice began to trail off as he answered, "One is in Florida, one lives in Georgia, and the other lives in Texas. I miss them and my grandchildren dearly."

Imani noticed the sad look in his eyes when he spoke of them. She smiled and said, "Well hey, they are some lucky ladies, to have a dad who is as wonderful as you are."

Mr. Sanchez smiled. "Well Imani, is there anything that I can do to help you?" He asked.

She was so grateful that he'd asked. "Well, I was wondering, if you needed any help around this place during the daytime? I know your brother Hector pretty much handles the evenings, so maybe I could do all of your shopping, and since I've been studying business in school, maybe I could also keep your records?"

Mr. Sanchez lifted his finger to his chin and paused. He seemed to give it some serious thought before he responded. "I guess I should have hired someone a long time ago, but the only problem is, I wouldn't have anything to do." He let out a soft chuckle.

Imani looked at him and said, "Well maybe you could start back golfing on a regular basis, go and visit your daughters and grandkids, or simply enjoy life. You said that when your wife Mary Ann died, a part of you died with her. You still have many years left ahead of you. I believe she'd want you to find happiness again outside of making everyone else happy."

He looked at Imani and said, "I swear you and my wife have the same heart. I know that's what she'd want. He gave Imani a friendly smile. "Well my friend, you've just landed yourself a job." Imani wore a broad smile; she couldn't be happier.

"Hold on now, don't get too excited because it comes with a stipulation," he said. Imani began to tone down her excitement. "What's the stipulation?" She asked.

Mr. Sanchez gave a soft smile, "You mustn't quit school."

Imani exhaled. "I think I can handle that."

Mr. Sanchez extended his hand. Imani looked down at his hand, paused for a few seconds before she extended hers. "Deal!" She said with an optimistic smile.

Mr. Sanchez walked Imani around the entire bar explaining many of the elements that went into running the establishment. They went over inventory, scheduling, payroll, and housekeeping. They also discussed her pay, her hours, and what her initial duties would be.

After their conversation, he scribbled down an address on a piece of paper. "I think I may have a place for you to rent. Meet me here tomorrow morning at ten am. After you take a look at the place, we'll meet back here, and I'll have a list of things for you to do."

Imani was bursting with excitement on the inside, but she remained calm on the outside. She didn't want to blow it.

They both stood up, and Mr. Sanchez extended his hand once more. For Imani, that wasn't good enough, so she stretched both her arms out wide and gave him a nice warm hug. Mr. Sanchez wasn't expecting that, but he hugged her back. Imani felt good. She needed that energy at that moment. So did Mr. Sanchez.

☙

LaShawn had the music on blast and was working in her studio when Imani stepped into her apartment. *"Thank goodness I won't have to be here much longer,"* Imani said to herself.

"Hey girl what's up?" Imani said yelling over the loud music. LaShawn was in full seamstress mode. She wore a tank top with a stoned scarf wrapped around her head, she had the sewing machine going, with her iron plugged, and the hot glue gun ready. Jean jackets, t-shirts, bras, beads, crystal stones, and patches, were all neatly organized on the table.

LaShawn stopped what she was doing and lowered the volume on the radio. “Hey Imani, I’m sorry, I didn’t go with you to look for a place today, but as you can tell, I’m swamped. I picked up so many orders last night until I don’t have time for myself. I have two weeks to complete this order and send it off to New York.” LaShawn said as she continued on with her work.

Imani looked at her friend and said, “I wish I could help, but I have no idea how to do any of that stuff. That certainly is your God-given talent and I have a feeling that this right here, will make you a rich lady.”

LaShawn said, “I sure hope so. Thanks for the offer but there is no need, I love doing this. I believe I work better under pressure.”

“That’s how they say diamonds are made,” Imani responded. LaShawn smiled and winked as she put her foot on the pedal of the sewing machine continuing her work.

Imani looked at her friend and said, “I appreciate you letting me stay here, I’m hoping to be out of here by the end of the week.”

LaShawn released her foot from the pedal and turned towards Imani. “Oh wow! That was fast. How did you pull that off?”

Imani was very careful and selective with her words because she wasn’t ready to tell all of her secrets, so she danced around the truth. "Well, the money that Mrs. Garrison gave me helped a lot. I put in applications at a few places that are closer to downtown. I should know something by tomorrow."

LaShawn nodded her head and said, "Well you go, girl."

Imani said, "I also stopped by the bar, and Mr. Sanchez has agreed to let me work there during the day. I'll be doing his bookkeeping and some other things. That works out better for me since the kids will be back soon, and we'll be on our own. The evening shift will be no good for me."

LaShawn looked surprised. "You sure you want to do that? Girl ain't no money up in that place during the daytime. Most people come in there and have a beer or a drink, and leave a small tip, and that's it. I love making money too much," she laughed.

Imani said, "Well it certainly won't be as much as I was making in the evening, but it will pay my bills. I have to look out for my family."

"Suit yourself," LaShawn replied.

଩

"The City of Grosse Pointe is a community nestled along the shore of Lake St. Clair. It's a place where lovely homes grace tree-lined streets." Imani studied the address given to her by Mr. Sanchez and decided that she'd need to have a backup plan. Grosse Pointe was a prestigious and affluent community, and she was sure that affordability would be an issue. But she decided to take the drive anyway. It definitely wouldn't hurt to take a look.

She hopped in her Jeep and rode the Lodge Freeway, exiting at E. Jefferson Avenue in Downtown Detroit. Imani loved riding through the streets of Downtown. It was considered a comeback city, and to see people moving out and about at Hart Plaza, the General Motors building, and Belle Isle, made her feel proud to have been raised in Detroit.

When she crossed over from Detroit into Grosse Pointe, the cities were noticeably different: Beautiful flowers lined the streets; the buildings looked fresher; the streets were cleaner, and the landscaping was impeccable. *"What a difference, one block makes."* Imani said to herself. Her excitement grew when the GPS told her to turn right, a half of a mile outside of Detroit. She didn't want to abandon the city altogether.

The street that she turned onto was nice, quiet, and neat, with huge older homes. At the end of the block, sat the Detroit River. Imani parked in front of the house and took in the beautiful scenery before strolling up to the door.

Mr. Sanchez answered on the first ring. He was kind and courteous as he welcomed her in. They both offered friendly smiles when they laid eyes on one another. Mr. Sanchez was a handsome man, and she couldn't help but notice how good he looked in casual attire. He had swapped out the Sanchez's lounge t-shirt and blue jeans for khaki pants, a white polo shirt, clean white canvas shoes, and a golf cap that fit his head nicely.

"Going golfing?" Imani asked as she stepped into the entryway of the home.

He smiled again and said, "Well I think I'll have a lot of extra time now that I have a new employee."

Mr. Sanchez retrieved a set of keys from his pocket and proceeded to open the door. "Imani, this house is a double unit. You have three bedrooms upstairs and three bedrooms downstairs. I'm going to show you the lower unit since the upstairs unit is occupied.

Imani eagerly waited as he unbolted the locks. She tried her best to relax, but that didn't last long once she was able to look inside. Imani inhaled deeply then exhaled as she placed both hands over her heart. The place needed no formal introduction; it was just perfect. "Oh Mr. Sanchez, I love it."

The partially furnished home had natural hardwood floors, a beautiful front bay window, a nice sized living, and dining area, an updated kitchen with stainless steel appliances, three bedrooms and one and a half baths.

She could hardly contain her excitement. She wanted to scream; "I'll take it." The only problem was, she didn't believe that she could afford such an extravagant place.

"Mr. Sanchez this place is so beautiful. I mean, it's perfect for my boys and me." Imani paused then let out a sigh. "But I'm afraid I can't afford it."

Mr. Sanchez was fond of her modesty. "I don't see how you can't afford it when you have a job." He said. Imani didn't quite comprehend what he was trying to say, so he started to explain.

"Imani, this unit has been unoccupied for close to three years. My daughter lived here up until she got married and moved to Florida. She took most of the furniture with her. I had planned on refurnishing the unit, but since they never come home to visit, I'm really in no rush."

Imani was even more confused. "Mr. Sanchez, I thought that you said your daughter lived with you up until she got married and moved away." He smiled at her.

She soon understood, "Oh I see. You live in the upstairs unit." His response was a meek, "Yes."

Mr. Sanchez said, "Imani, I've been helping people all my life. I see how hard you work and the love that you have for your children. I believe this place is perfect for them, and the school systems in this area are great. If you keep your promise and stay in school, you can work for me and rent this place at a fair rate. I'm certain your pay will cover it."

Imani took a quick full breath. She was shocked. *This just doesn't happen.* She said to herself.

He went on to say, "School is a big deal for me. Everybody is not cut out for it, but I know you are. Two out of three of my daughters graduated from college with honors. My youngest wasn't that great in school, so she obtained a realtor's license. She lucked up and sold her first million-dollar home to a baseball star. Six months later she was engaged to him, and now they're happily married."

"Mr. Sanchez I really can't thank you enough for this offer. I have no idea what I did to deserve such mercy, but I can't accept this. I need to pay my own way. I don't want anyone putting me out, ever again." She said.

"Your modesty is what makes me want to help you even more. "Don't worry; you will pay your own way. I have a leasing agreement that you'll have to sign. Mr. Sanchez said.

She hesitated for a few seconds, "Mr. Sanchez, you just made me an offer that I can't refuse." Imani stretched her arms out wide and gave Mr. Sanchez a tight hug. He smiled simply at the gesture. Imani decided to take it a step further and follow it up with a soft kiss on his cheek. He was caught by surprise.

"Imani that's not necessary. You didn't have to do that."

She looked at him with an earnest smile and said, "I know that. It's something I wanted to do."

To Imani the kiss wasn't staged, contrived, or rehearsed; it just felt natural to her, so she took a chance. She had no regrets. Mr. Sanchez was her definition of a real man, just like her father. They shared some of the same qualities: both were strong men who knew how to lead. That's what she was missing in her life. Imani knew that she was born different, perhaps from another time and era. She felt as though she had more in common with Mr. Sanchez than she did with men her age. Although she tried her best to make the relationship with Brandon work, she now knew it was never meant to be. Other than their children, they really had nothing in common.

Imani's kiss seemed to put Mr. Sanchez on a cloud. He was completely mesmerized. He just stood there speechless, unsure of what to do next.

Imani snapped him out of it. "Are you going to show me the rest of the house?"

He cleared his throat. "Follow me."

Mr. Sanchez gave Imani a tour of the house and the entire area. He explained that he and his wife bought the house thirty years ago, raised their children in the home, and had planned to spend the rest of their lives there.

He escorted her up the stairs to his home. Imani noticed that Mr. Sanchez's home mirrored the lower unit, except it, was filled with much more family memorabilia. It was warm and comforting. One could almost feel the presence of his beautiful late wife, Mary Ann. One could tell that, from the family photos that lined the walls, the Sanchez's appeared to be the picture-perfect family.

Mary Ann was a short, thin, woman, who had long beautiful black hair and a lovely smile. Their three daughters were all just as beautiful. But what surprised Imani the most were the dates on the photos; his daughters were only a few years older than her.

Mr. Sanchez led Imani to his music room. Imani smiled to herself, as she didn't know a man who didn't have a music collection. But Mr. Sanchez's room was different. It was very personal, warm and inviting. It reminded you more of a musical shrine. He and Mrs. Sanchez had traveled all over the world and had taken photos with many celebrities.

Imani carefully looked at each photo and became utterly star-struck. The picture with The Sanchez's standing with B.B. King in front of B.B. King's restaurant had to have been one of her favorites. There were also autographed framed photos of the couple standing alongside Patti LaBelle, Aretha Franklin, Elton John, Carlos Santana, and many others.

Mr. Sanchez eyes suddenly became melancholy. "Imani, I hardly ever sit in this room. It's too painful. It reminds me of the good old days, and I long for those days." He said in a sad and somber voice.

The soft tone of his words caused Imani to feel his pain. "Well Mr. Sanchez, let's liven this room back up and get the party started. I grew up listening to all this stuff with my dad. I'll take the blues, jazz, Motown, or the 80's over rap music any day." She said trying her best to uplift his spirits.

Mr. Sanchez was shocked. "You mean you really know about this stuff?" He asked quizzically.

Imani responded, "Heck yeah! My father's CD/record collection is in his basement, and it's off limits to everyone." She laughed. "I loved sitting downstairs with him every Saturday morning as he sorted his records, Cassette tapes, and CDs. We'd have our own party in that basement. Even though he now has a digital audio system, those CD's are still off limits."

Imani pulled out a Johnnie Taylor CD, and handed it to Mr. Sanchez. "Can you play Last Two Dollars' please?" She said wearing a big smile across her face.

Mr. Sanchez chuckled hard and said, "Why sure." He inserted the CD. Imani's mouth and eyes both widened with glee once she heard the beat of the music. She was feeling good as one of her, and her dad's favorite songs began to croon through the speakers. She started singing, clapping her hands, bobbing her head, rocking her body, patting her feet, as the song played.

When the song reached the chorus, she balled her fist and used it as a microphone as she sang... *"But these last two dollars, I'm not gonna lose. These last two dollars, I'm not gonna lose..."* This was a happy moment for Imani. She jumped around and began pointing, and laughing, and playing the "air" guitar for Mr. Sanchez like she was being paid.

Mr. Sanchez was enjoying the show. They both laughed and smiled so hard until they had tears.

When the song had ended, Mr. Sanchez said, "Imani, I haven't had a good laugh like that since Mary Ann passed away. She and I both shared the love of music, and it hasn't been the same without her."

Mr. Sanchez didn't want the party to end. He began to play some of his favorite artists, which included Dianna Ross, Marvin Gaye, Stevie Wonder, and Carlos Santana. Imani loved it. They spent the next few hours in that room listening to music and enjoying each other's company.

Once their mini-concert ended, Mr. Sanchez provided Imani a tour of the entire house and property.

Her other favorite place was the backyard. It was spacious. It had a garden, a small pond and was surrounded by tall trees. Her boys would have plenty of room to play. Mr. Sanchez walked her to the end of the block where the Detroit River sat. There was a park bench where she could sit back and enjoy the view. The place was just lovely.

Imani signed the lease agreement and was given the keys that afternoon.

She was grateful for Mr. Sanchez. The fact that he'd opened up his home to her and her boys would never be forgotten. He was a real man. That's just what she needed in her life, a real man.

☙

The next three days of Imani's life could be described in three words, "A beautiful mess." For the first time in years, Imani felt so alive. It felt good to be needed and appreciated by someone other than her children.

It was beautiful because she loved her new place and didn't want to leave. After she'd signed the leasing agreement, Mr. Sanchez handed her the keys and a bottle of red wine as a house-warming gift. He left her alone so that she could become acclimated to her new surroundings. He even extended the invitation to his music room. "Imani, if you ever want to go up and listen to music in my room, you're more than welcome to do so." She couldn't be happier as she was looking forward to going up those stairs and blasting Stephanie Mills song "Home."

Since Imani now had a debit card, she ordered everything she needed for her place online and opted for overnight shipping.

She ordered beds for the boys and herself, shower curtains, towels, sheets, rugs, and other small appliances. She set the place up all by herself. It was beautiful and coming together nicely.

Her life was also a mess, because of all the lies she had to tell, secrets she had to keep, and the phone calls she had to avoid. She lied to her parents and avoided LaShawn. Having a place of her own was special, and she didn't want anyone to spoil it for her.

She and Mr. Sanchez bonded over those days, as they had to work closely together. He taught her how to do basic bookkeeping, order supplies, take inventory and maintenance. Mr. Sanchez was proud, as he witnessed how tirelessly she'd worked on her new place, and at the bar with him. She hardly got any rest. But he couldn't help but take notice of the glow in her eyes, and the huge smile that was now a part of her make-up.

Mr. Sanchez decided that he wanted to do something nice for her to reward her for all the hard work she'd done.

After they'd wrapped up the bar at the end of the fourth day, he handed her an envelope. "Here's your pay." She stared at the envelope and before she could question, he said, "No questions, your hard work hasn't gone unnoticed."

Mr. Sanchez added, "I want you to go home and get dressed because I'd like to take you out to dinner this evening."

Imani smiled, "I'd love to, but there's so much I haven't taken care of around here."

He looked at her and gently said, "Imani that's not a question."

Imani suddenly dropped everything she was doing and said, “You got it, Mr. Sanchez.”

Mr. Sanchez stopped her again, “Imani, since we are now friends, please feel free to call me Carlos.”

Imani was beaming as she said, “Carlos, I'll be ready in an hour.”

☙

The restaurant was located on a golf course in Bloomfield Hills. It was an elegant, upscale place, with beautiful chandeliers, a piano bar, a waterfall that sat in the center, and a wine cellar that must have had over a hundred varieties of wine.

When Carlos and Imani entered the restaurant, a young waitress greeted them at the door and introduced herself. Before the waitress could escort them over to a table, a tall, beautiful, lean, older woman with long dark hair, wearing all black and draped in expensive diamonds, interrupted the waitress. “I'll seat these guests,” She said, quickly dismissing the young waitress.

The older woman's face lit up once she laid eyes on Carlos.

“Carlos,” she smiled as she extended her arms offering him hug. Carlos returned the smile and reciprocated her embrace.

"It's so good to see you. George and I were just talking about you. We'd planned to pop in at your establishment since you don't come around to see us anymore." The woman said still smiling.

Carlos gave a friendly smile and said, "Janice, I miss you and George as well. It's been rough the past couple of years, so I've been keeping myself busy with work."

Janice nodded her head up and down and said, "I truly understand."

Carlos introduced Imani. "Janice I'd like you to meet my "life-saver." Her name is Imani McNair. She's been working for me for a few months, and I swear she's just what I needed. Imani here is a great listener, sincere, a fast learner, and pretty soon she'll be running Sanchez's all by herself." Carlos gave a warm smile. "Janice, you and George just may be seeing a lot more of me." He said.

Janice was friendly. She offered a gracious smile and shook Imani's hand. "I'm so pleased to meet you, my dear."

Janice retrieved two menus, nodded her head and said, "Please follow me this way."

She sat them at a table in perfect view of the piano bar. "Carlos, I'll send George out, shortly, he's going to be so happy to see you. Also, everything is on us. We've missed you." She said with sincerity.

Carlos ordered a bottle of red wine. Imani couldn't contain her excitement. "You have some very generous friends." She said in awe.

He looked a bit somber. "Yes, they're great people. George and I go way back. I was his best man when he married Janice, and he was my best man when I married Mary Ann. When she passed away, I pulled back from the things Mary Ann and I shared, out of sadness and threw myself into my work. Lately, I've been doing much better. I can't say that the pain will ever go away, but I now know, it does get easier."

Imani let out a soft smile as she rubbed his hand. "I couldn't even imagine."

Carlos began to perk up as he sipped his wine. "I didn't bring you here to talk about me; I brought you here to talk about you."

Imani's eyebrows rose as he spoke. "These past four days, you have been working extremely hard nonstop and I've noticed that you've hardly gotten any rest and you haven't talked to anyone, including your parents." Before she could respond, he reached inside his pocket and retrieved her cell phone. She became alarmed.

"Imani, you left this phone on top of the bar three days ago, and you haven't even inquired about it. I would never purposely look through anyone's phone, but I couldn't help but notice you had several missed calls from your parents." As Carlos handed her the phone, he said; "The battery even died, they called so much."

Imani looked down with sadness in her eyes. She was happy for the first time, in a long time. If she had called her parents, they would have most likely spoiled it.

Carlos extended his finger and lifted her chin. “I know you said, you want to do this on your own, but please don’t alienate everyone. I’m a parent, and if my daughters didn’t call me regularly, I’d be so hurt. They only want what’s best for you. I’m sure they mean no harm.”

Imani shook her head meekly. “I planned on calling them; I just wanted to have this time to myself. I have about a week left before my boys will be back and I just wanted to make sure I had things together without any distractions.”

He smiled, “I understand. That’s why I’m insisting you take tomorrow off, so you can go and put your parents’ mind at ease. You cannot hide forever. You’re a brilliant woman, you’ll think of something.”

Imani began to blush. “Yes, I will.”

Imani and Carlos enjoyed the rest of the evening listening to the dulcet tones of jazz at the restaurant. His friends George and Janice joined their table. They were so happy to see Carlos that they never bothered to question his and Imani’s relationship. That made Imani feel good.

When Carlos and Imani returned home, they each went to their separate places. Imani did wish that Carlos would have come and sat with her for a while, but she knew it was too soon. Imani loved his company, and he was a great storyteller, so she would learn to be patient. *"Good things come to those who wait."* At least that's what she'd been taught.

Imani retrieved her phone from her purse and plugged it into the wall. After about ten minutes it lit up. She held the power button until it shut down. She was going to enjoy this evening alone without any stress.

She smiled as she poured herself a glass of wine. "A toast to new beginnings." She said to herself as she sipped the wine in peace.

ଓ

Imani stared at the ceiling for a few minutes before her feet hit the floor. She was thinking of how peaceful the past few days of her life had been. In about a week, her life would change again. Her boys would be home, and she would have to shift back into "*mommy mode.*" She looked forward to it.

But first, she'd have to get through today. She knew it would be a real challenge, but she couldn't put it off any longer. She'd mapped out her day in her head. She decided that she'd see LaShawn first. She was going to sit down with her girlfriend and tell her the truth. She was happy with her life, and she hoped her friend would be happy for her as well.

She decided that she'd see her parents last. Once she went to their house, they'd probably hold her hostage since she'd been missing in action for so long.

As she proceeded to get dressed, she turned her phone on. Her voice mail was flooded with calls from her parents. She took a deep breath and decided to give her mom a call while her father was at work.

She punched in the number. Her mother answered on the first ring. "Imani," she said in a relieved voice. "I've been calling you nonstop for the past few days." Before Imani could respond, her father snatched the phone from her mother. "Imani!" He yelled. "Your mother has been worried sick about you. I took off work today because she has begged me to go looking for you. You have a lot of explaining to do young lady." He yelled.

Imani let out a heavy sigh, as she heard her mother plead, "Pete, please don't talk to her that way, you'll make her run away again." Her father paid her mother no mind, as he continued to fuss. "If you don't get over here and explain to us what's going on, you don't ever have to worry about coming here again." She heard her mother yell at him, "Pete don't say that." By that time, Imani had heard enough. She ended the phone.

Imani bowed her head and started shaking. She knew her father was upset and that he really didn't mean that, however she wasn't a child. She was a woman who paid her own bills and her own way. She crossed her parent's home from her list of places to visit today; she'd see them next week when the kids returned.

ꕤ

LaShawn's friend De'Andre was leaving as Imani was arriving. "Hello Imani, it's nice to see you again. Your girl LaShawn is upstairs tripping because I'm leaving town again. Maybe you can help her understand that if I don't work, I won't be able to take care of her someday." He said.

"Well as you can tell, LaShawn isn't hurting for money. What she's looking for, money cannot buy." Imani snapped back as she folded her arms awaiting his response.

He had none. Instead, he gave Imani a frustrated look, let out a heavy sigh and said, "Have a nice day."

Imani tapped on LaShawn's door instead of using her key. She didn't want to alarm her. LaShawn yelled from the other side of the door, "Did you forget something De'Andre? I told you I'd had enough of this dead-end relationship?"

Imani snickered. "LaShawn, he's gone, it's me Imani."

LaShawn snatched the door open. "And where the hell have you been for the last few days?" She took one look at Imani and saw how vibrant and happy she appeared. Oh never mind. I see you and Brandon have rekindled the flame because you look great. I hope that it works out for you two because you deserve to be happy. It's so hard to find a good mate these days."

Imani took a deep breath, "LaShawn, how about we make some breakfast and sip some tea. I haven't been completely honest with you my friend." LaShawn looked alarmed.

Before Imani said another word, she extended her pinkie finger. LaShawn began to smile as she locked her pinky finger with her Imani's." LaShawn knew what that meant. It was something serious and was only to be discussed between the two.

LaShawn's mouth hung open the entire time as Imani spoke the truth.

"LaShawn, I haven't been happy for a very long time. Brandon and I had a big fight over his love for the video game. I packed my things and ran to my parent's home at four o'clock in the morning. I knew that I couldn't stay there because my father is still so controlling, so I decided to go back to Brandon and try to work it out. That didn't happen because Brandon had the locks changed, leaving me homeless. I was so angry that I went to his job and damaged his car. I then busted him with his co-worker, and I completely lost it. To sum this all up, I narrowly escaped catching a criminal case."

Lashawn was floored. "Oh no! So that's why you were bleeding? You mean to tell me that you held all of that in for the past few days?" She said in total shock.

Imani shrugged. "I was too humiliated and embarrassed to talk about it."

LaShawn reached in and gave her friend a huge embrace. "I'm so sorry you had to go through that alone. You know that you could have told me. Please remember that we go way back. I'll always be here for you." Lashawn said with sincerity.

Imani's eyes became glassy. She appreciated the gesture. "Thank you. I know you will."

After they exchanged hugs and tears, LaShawn paused. "Well wait a minute. What's up with this sudden glow? Is there something else you should tell me?"

Imani started laughing. "Dang! I thought I'd save that for another time, but I see you caught me." They both giggled.

Imani extended her pinky finger again. LaShawn rolled her eyes with sarcasm as she locked fingers with her friend once again.

"Ok LaShawn, this is serious. I haven't even told my parents about this." Imani said, with a stone face.

Imani let out a deep breath and hesitated for a few seconds. She began to smile, as she looked up with starry eyes. "He's a wonderful, wonderful, human being. He's sweet, kind, non-judgmental, compassionate, considerate, rich, generous, handsome…

LaShawn cut her off. "Well Damn! What planet did he come from, and does he have a brother?"

Imani continued to look up and smile. She let out another deep breath and hesitated for several more seconds. "His name is Carlos Sanchez."

LaShawn returned her smile. "Ok, he sounds like he's…" When suddenly, LaShawn realized who her handsome prince was. LaShawn took a full gasp. She held it for several seconds before saying, "Oh my God, Mr. Sanchez!"

Imani let out a sheepish grin as she slowly nodded her head up and down.

LaShawn couldn't help but ask, "How in the hell did that happen? I mean, he is fine for an older man, but doesn't that feel weird? He's old enough to be your father. I mean, don't you want to be with a guy that's closer to your age?"

Imani laughed, "No it doesn't feel weird, and nothing has happened between us yet. He's been a pure gentleman. I love his company, he's a great listener, and we have so much in common." She said trying to sound convincing.

LaShawn stiffened her neck and pursed her lips together. "Oh really? Well, what is it that you two have in common?" Lashawn asked, not completely sold on the relationship.

Imani began to boast. "We love the same music, we're both laid back, and we're both single. Besides, older men are settled, and they don't play games. I don't have time for that anymore. I like for my man to know already what he wants."

Imani rolled her neck and said, "I'm happy you got rid of De'Andre, he's just like Brandon, a boy. LaShawn you should probably find you an older man. You know what they say? Don't knock it until you try it."

LaShawn's was in shock. She'd never seen this side of Imani before. *'Where in the hell did this come from she wondered."* She was at a loss for words. *Imani only had one relationship that she knew of, and now that she'd hooked up with the boss, she suddenly felt like she had all the answers.* LaShawn kept quiet and just listened intently as Imani told her about her new place, and the job.

LaShawn had heard enough. "Imani, stop right there! This is a bit much! What if this relationship doesn't work? Where would that leave you?" She ask curiously.

Imani was so confident, that she refused to entertain negative thoughts. "Broke and homeless." She joked.

LaShawn didn't laugh. "Imani, I'm not finding this funny."

Imani huffed. "Carlos and I went over all of those things. I can assure you that I'll be fine. I'm dealing with a real man. He pays me a salary, and I even signed a year lease agreement. LaShawn for the first time, I'm paying my own way." She said in a hubristic tone.

LaShawn shook her head with skepticism. “Carlos?” She said with a bit of a laugh. “Well since you guys are on a first name basis, then I guess there’s nothing that I can say. “Ok. I hope you know what you’re doing.”

LaShawn added, “Oh, and I’ll pass on the old men. I like them young and tender.” Lashawn said undoubtedly.

Imani nodded her head. “Suit yourself. I’m done with that road.” She said boldly.

LaShawn tried her best to stay positive, so she said, “Well I’d love to stop by and see your new place.”

Imani responded, “I’d love that too.”

LaShawn grabbed her floppy hat, and oversized sunglasses and said, “Well cool, help me drop these boxes off at the post office, and we’ll go shopping and then swing by your new place.”

☙

LaShawn and Imani spent the entire day shopping, eating, drinking and having some good old fashion girl time. LaShawn purchased Imani throw pillows, silk flowers, picture frames, and other trinkets to make her place feel like a home.

As they loaded the items into Imani’s Jeep, LaShawn said, “Imani I know how it feels when you move into a new place, it's kind of sad, dreary and depressing. The items that I purchased for you would bring life to any home."

Imani responded, "I appreciate this because I've never had an eye for the small details." She smiled at her friend. "You're the best LaShawn."

As Imani exited Detroit and crossed over into Grosse Pointe, LaShawn glared at Imani and asked, "where in the hell are you going?" Imani didn't answer, she continued to smile until they arrived at their destination.

"Welcome to my new place." Imani said with a look of pride.

LaShawn was aghast. "Are you kidding me? Grosse Pointe? Really?" She said in disbelief.

When they entered the home, LaShawn quickly dropped the bags and threw her hands up and said, enthusiastically, "Oh. My. God. Look at you!"

Imani smiled while doing a ballerina spin. "You like?" She asked, Lashawn.

"Hell yea I like it." Lashawn said.

"Let me give you the grand tour." said Imani.

LaShawn was awestruck. "Girl, you have new furniture, stainless steel appliances, these beautiful floors, and one and a half baths. "You struck gold." She said.

Imani strutted around her new home proud. "I sure did." She said boastfully. "Now let me go grab a bottle of wine, so we can celebrate my accomplishments." Imani said.

Imani and LaShawn spent the next couple of hours sipping wine, decorating and talking about Imani's new life. But as the wine began to take its effect, the mood started to change. Imani realized that she seemed to be doing most of the talking. LaShawn became quiet as she continued to look around Imani's home, in awe!

After the girls finished up the second bottle of wine, Imani went to the kitchen to retrieve another bottle. When she returned, she noticed LaShawn gathering up her things.

"LaShawn, where are you going? I wanted to open up another bottle."

"No, I've had enough. I better get going because I don't want to run into Mr Sanchez, oh, I mean Carlos." She said in a mocking tone.

Imani was disappointed, her friend's snide remark didn't sit well with her.

LaShawn then shook her head and sighed. "You and Mr. Sanchez, that just doesn't even sound right." she said.

Imani looked at her friend and said, "LaShawn I brought you here because I thought you'd be happy for me."

Lashawn looked over at Imani and said, "Imani, if you like it then I love it." Lashawn then offered a smile.

Imani sighed, deciding to let it go. She could see right through LaShawn's smile, it was phony. LaShawn was failing miserably at pretending to be happy for her. Imani sensed that LaShawn was jealous. Imani just didn't understand why. She'd celebrated LaShawn and all of her accomplishments throughout the years, and Imani believed that she deserved the same. "Wow!" LaShawn had turned into a *hater*." Imani thought to herself.

LaShawn felt the tension, "Imani, stop it with the long face, you just sprang all of this on me today. It feels sort of creepy to me. I mean he is still our boss." She said.

Imani hunched her shoulders, "It's cool. Just let me grab my keys, and I'll drop you back off at your place."

"Girl that's ok. We've both been drinking. I'll call an Uber." LaShawn said as she rushed to gather up her things.

Within ten minutes, LaShawn's ride was outside. She could hardly look Imani in the eyes as they exchanged good-byes.

Imani brushed it off. She had lived by other's rules and their expectations her entire life. She was done with that. This was about her and her children. She was proud of herself for what she'd accomplished, and it was worthy of praise.

Imani filled another glass of wine and toasted up to herself.

ᴕ

The days were moving fast, and the countdown had begun. Imani awoke early, dressed, had a cup of tea, and began to check her daily notes. As she prepared to head out, there was a light tapping on her door. She felt giddy, as she knew it was Carlos.

"Good Morning Imani, did you enjoy your day off?" Carlos said.

She gave a relaxed smile, "It was wonderful, and I even spoke to my parents." She said, hoping that he didn't want any details.

"That's great." He then said, "Imani I was heading out for brunch, would you like to join me?"

Imani could not have been more delighted, "Of course I would. I'm starved."

ᴕ

The restaurant was a nice, cool, hip spot that sat off the Detroit River. The boat docking station, cabanas, and patio lounge made for a relaxed environment. The day was warm and sunny, so Carlos and Imani opted for patio seating.

Once they were seated, Imani couldn't help but stare and admire how everyone seemed so carefree. An older couple was docking their boat, a few people were hanging out in the cabanas, and a few others were sipping mimosas at the bar.

Imani suddenly closed her eyes and relaxed. She slowly inhaled and then slowly exhaled. She slowly inhaled, and then slowly exhaled. She did this several more times as she wanted to savor the moment.

Imani understood that this wasn't her real life. For her, real life consisted of small needy children, play dates, and sleepless nights. The life she was now living was temporary and seemed like more of a fantasy. In a few days, the temporary status would revert to permanent, and this fantasy would come to an end. Her life as a single parent would begin. Days like this would be *few and far between*. She could feel Carlos staring at her, but she didn't care. Imani deemed it necessary to take it all in.

"Carlos, this is the happiest I've been in a very long time. Thank you for showing me what I've been missing out on, for so long. Thank you for giving me the opportunity to make it on my own, and thank you for being so kind."

Carlos stopped her. For it was she, whom he believed, deserved all the praise and accolades. "No

Imani, thank you for being my friend. These past few months since I've met you, you have given my life hope and new meaning. I've learned that it's ok to take care of others, and yourself as well. You have helped me to understand that I don't have to stop living, or feeling guilty about living because my wife is gone. I am not completely there yet, but I am confident, I will eventually get there. I know that Mary Ann will always be with me." Carlos then lowered his head and touched his heart.

Imani rubbed his free hand and said, "Carlos, you're doing great. Yes, she will always be with you."

After they'd finished their breakfast, Carlos reached inside his pocket and retrieved four tickets. "Imani, I have two sets of tickets, to two separate events. I'd love to take you to this blues concert at the Fox Theatre tomorrow evening."

Imani didn't have to think about it. "Of course, I'll go, you know that I love the blues."

Carlos gave an appreciative smile. "I haven't been to a concert in many years, and I'm looking forward to this. I want us to paint the town."

Imani laughed. "I can't wait."

She then questioned, "What other tickets do you have?"

Carlos studied the tickets. "Walk Fashion Show." It was founded right here in the city of Detroit. The show is the day after tomorrow. I figured that you and

LaShawn would like to attend." He said while handing over the tickets to Imani.

"Wow! LaShawn would love this. That girl lives for fashion. I know that you'll probably be short on staff, so I'll cover for her." Imani said while sliding the tickets into her purse.

Imani had no plans to attend, as she remembered what happened the last time she went to an event with LaShawn.

ꕥ

Imani couldn't stop staring at herself in the trifold mirror at Macy's department store. The little black dress and black pumps fit her perfectly, but she looked too conservative. She wanted to break away from her norm. This date with Carlos was special, so Imani wanted to be a little more daring without being sleazy.

Imani did a right pivot so that she could catch sight of what she looked like from the side. "Carlos was right; she didn't have much back there."

Imani took each of her hands and placed them under her buttocks and gently lifted both cheeks. "Wow!" She said to herself, the dress looked much better with a protruding buttock. She turned to face forward in the mirror and looked down at her small "A" cups. She placed both hands under her breast and lifted until her cleavage peaked through the dress. She liked that look.

Imani suddenly relaxed and stared at herself in the mirror once more, but this time she wasn't alone. She quickly ducked her head in embarrassment, as the female sales associate stood several feet behind her holding undergarments.

The older shapely black woman gave Imani a soft smile and said, "Young lady you don't have to feel embarrassed about trying to modify your figure, we all do it."

Imani relaxed, hunched her shoulders and laughed.

The woman held up a one-piece undergarment that she'd specifically picked out for Imani. "This right here is called a body shaper. It has soft padding for your bottom and soft padding for your top while holding everything together. It will definitely give you the lift that you're after.

Imani picked the garment up and said, "Do you have one with bigger butt pads?"

The older lady let out a hearty laugh. "Young lady, you have a beautiful small frame, so you don't need all of that. This here body shaper is subtle and natural, and it enhances what you already have. Butt pads, in my opinion, are just wrong. They look so unnatural. I've even witnessed them shift while being worn."

The woman added, "Young lady, just keep on living. In due time, you will fill out. One day you'll wake up and wonder what happened. You will then wish that you could give some of that thickness back." She then said, "Hmpppp, I know I sure do."

Imani gave a gracious smile, as she was very appreciative that the woman had taken the time out to offer her honest advice about her body. She wished that she could have gone to her mom, but for obvious reasons, she couldn't.

Since the price was no longer a factor, Imani purchased all of the items. She left out of Macy's feeling good and confident.

☙

LaShawn had promised Imani that she'd be ready for her at four o'clock. It was close to five o'clock, and Imani's hair hadn't been shampooed. She wasn't surprised, as this was the way LaShawn did business when it came to her. Imani never had any real plans, and LaShawn never charged her much, so she technically had no right to complain. But today, Imani had plans, she had money, and she didn't have time to wait.

Imani stepped over to LaShawn's hair station and said with an attitude, "I have a date tonight, so I have to get going. How much longer do you think I'll have to wait?"

LaShawn rolled her eyes and huffed, just as Imani handed her the tickets to the fashion show along with a hundred dollars. “This is complimentary from Carlos.”

LaShawn accepted the tickets and the cash. Her huff quickly turned into a cheerful smile when she realized the tickets were for “Walk” fashion show. Her smile turned even wider once she read the words, “Runway seating.”

“Imani, these tickets are for premier seating.” She screamed. “I get to experience this up close and personal. I’ve followed “Walk” for a long time. They have shows across several states, including Atlanta and New York. I’m so excited! Tell Mr. Sanchez I said thank you!”

LaShawn called out to her assistant and said, “Please get Imani washed and prepped immediately, she has to get out of here.”

In a little over an hour, LaShawn handed Imani the mirror.

Imani smiled. She loved her hair, her eyebrows, and makeup, but most of all she loved the priority service.

LaShawn whispered in her ear as she slid the money back to her. “You don’t have to give me anything; the tickets were enough. Oh, I’m so sorry to have kept you waiting. I forgot you’ve switched leagues.” She said with a hint of sarcasm.

ꙮ

The sales associate at Macy's was correct. The body shaper hugged her small frame perfectly. It enhanced her bottom half and her top half, making it appear as though she had an hourglass figure.

But Imani couldn't hold back the laughs as she looked down at the body shaper. It reminded her of her mother.

Imani remembered being a small girl, sitting on the edge of her mother's bed, as her mother dressed for an evening out with her father. "Imani hand me my girdle." Her mother would step into the girdle and pull, and tug until everything fit smoothly. The more Imani looked at the body shaper, the more she realized, that the body shaper was nothing but a fancier name, for a girdle.

Imani had approximately ten minutes to be ready before Carlos would come tapping on her door. She didn't know why, but she was so nervous. She frantically ran through her house sweating, panting, and fanning herself.

She finally forced herself to slow down. "*Relax Imani, Breath Imani, slow down Imani.*"

She didn't understand; it wasn't as if this was the first time they'd been out. They'd been on several dates, but this date would be different. It wasn't impromptu like the others. She had time to plan. Carlos had told her that he wanted to paint the town, so Imani went out of her way to look her best. She'd hoped that he'd notice and she'd prayed that she hadn't overdone it.

The sales associate at Macy's referring to her as "young lady," bothered her. She would have preferred to have been called ma'am, but that didn't happen. Imani knew she was young. *But did she look that young? Would she really look like she was going out with her father?* That's why she had LaShawn, spiral curl her hair. She wanted it to look a bit edgy, grown, or maybe even sexy. Imani had ditched the soft lip-gloss and traded it for hot red. She made sure that she took her time applying it.

Imani believed the little black dress looked stunning on her. She felt like a knockout. Whenever she and Brandon would go out, they both dressed casually; it worked for both of them. But now Imani was in an entirely different league. She had a man. A real grown man and she enjoyed every minute of it.

Imani heard the tapping at the door.

She took a deep breath and exhaled. She ran her fingers through her hair once more in an attempt to add more sex appeal. She dabbed a little perfume behind her ears, on her neck, and between her cleavage. She wanted Carlos to view her as a grown woman, and not the "young lady" the sales associate believed her to be.

Imani took several deep breaths before she was able to calm herself. She put one hand on the knob and struck a pose as she opened the door.

Imani's stomach did somersaults as he stood there looking like he belonged to the Puerto Rican Mafia. It wasn't that she wanted a mafia man, she just thought that they dressed so cool. Carlos wore black dress pants and jacket, a white button-down shirt with no tie, and a black fedora hat.

That hat is what did it for her. Although they looked nothing alike, he reminded her of Peter McNair. Her father loves those hats. Every Father's Day, she'd ride downtown with her mother to Henry the Hatter, and select a *fedora* hat for her father. She liked the way her father looked in those hats, and she liked the way Carlos looked in his.

Carlos just stood there staring at Imani with a bottle of wine in his hand. It was apparent that he'd noticed the change in her, and according to his eyes, he liked what he saw.

"Imani!" Carlos said nearly out of breath. "You look breathtaking. Gorgeous. Amazing. I apologize in advance if my stares make you uncomfortable, but I can't help myself.

Imani blushed, "Carlos, you look amazing as well. I love the hat. You said that you wanted to paint the town, so let's start painting."

Carlos flashed a happy smile, "I've hired a driver, and he'll be here in ten minutes. Let's have a toast before we go."

Imani and Carlos held up two glasses of red wine, while Carlos led the toast. "A toast to good times."

ᏅᏰ

The concert was nothing short of spectacular. Imani and Carlos had front row seats, and for her, it was quite the experience. Imani didn't care that she was one of the youngest faces in the crowd either. She clapped and sang every song along with the artists. Carlos had a wide smile painted on his face. He seemed to have had more enjoyment watching Imani than the actual the show. The entire evening was one for the record books.

After the concert, they had dinner at a nice restaurant inside the casino. They pulled a few slots, listened to more great music, and enjoyed more wine.

The evening had finally come to a close. Carlos and Imani slowly strolled to the door, as they both weren't quite ready to part ways. Carlos opened the entrance door, and Imani stepped inside. Before she inserted her key into the door, she turned to face Carlos and stared deep into his eyes as she spoke with sincerity. "Thank you for this wonderful evening. It's one that I will cherish for a very long time."

Carlos took a deep breath, as he couldn't take his eyes off of her. She was simply beautiful. He reached out and held her hands.

He spoke haltingly, "Imani, you are one special lady." He then let out a long sigh, closed his eyes and repeated, "Definitely one special lady!"

Imani couldn't deny that there was strong chemistry and attraction between the two of them. Hand holding was no longer enough for her. She hadn't been touched in a while. She wanted more. She needed more. Imani freed her hands, pressed her body against Carlos's, and wrapped her arms around his neck. It was as if they were one. Their soft breathing, and strong heartbeats in sync, creating a melody that only the two of them could quite possibly understand. Imani stood tall on the balls of her feet, totally intoxicated by the smell of his masculine aroma. "Mmmmm" she whispered as Carlos rested his hands along the small of her back. Imani tilted her head seductively to one side, as Carlos swiftly lifted her tiny body into the air. *And It was at that very moment that Imani felt relieved that she had opted out of the butt pads.*

For several seconds their lips locked into a passionate kiss, before they slowly disengaged. The mood was intense for both of them. The energy and attraction between the two was palpable, but they both knew it was too soon to throw caution to the wind and take that next step.

Imani felt like she was ready, but she had to be absolutely certain. Her children would be home in a few days, and whatever relationship she and Carlos had, would have to be put on hold. She was a dedicated mother before anything else, and she had no idea what to expect when they returned. This new world to them would be foreign, and she wanted to make the transition for them as smooth, and as comfortable as possible.

Imani also hoped and prayed that she could find a way to have both. She was not ready to give up on the possibility of being with Carlos and the wonderful life she believed he could provide for her and her children.

ଓ

Imani went to bed with a lot on her mind. She dreamed about having a loving, blended family with Carlos, and both families being accepting of the relationship.

She could vividly see the wedding, her gown, the flowers, her sons as ring bearers, his daughters as her bridesmaids and her father escorting her down the aisle. She was excited as her "Prince" stood at the altar wearing a white suit waiting for her. But the dream was strange, as her Prince's face was just a blur. As she and her father approached the altar, Imani's phone buzzed, and her dream was disrupted.

"Damn!" She said.

Imani looked over at the clock, and it was after two am. She stumbled out of bed and grabbed her purse. Her heart pounded as she had five missed calls and five text messages, all from Brandon. He'd sent the last text, fifteen minutes ago. She became nervous since he hadn't called in over a week. The only thing she could think of was something being wrong with her children.

She quickly skimmed the messages…

The first text message came in at eleven o'clock pm, and it read: "Hi."

The second text message came fifteen minutes later, and it read: "We need to talk?"

The third message came in at twelve a.m., and it read: "Where are you?"

The fourth message came in at twelve thirty a.m., and it read: "I just left your job, and that smart mouth LaShawn laughed in my face and said she hadn't seen you. I know she's lying."

The fifth message came in at one fifteen, and it read: "Imani, it's about the kids?"

Imani immediately dialed Brandon's number. He answered on the first ring.

"Hello Imani," he said in a subdued voice. "I see you finally called me back."

She was angry and felt this had nothing to do with the kids, but she remained calm.

"Brandon, what's wrong with the boys?"

He responded in a somber voice. "Oh, so you really don't care how I'm doing? You weren't going to call back unless I said it was about the boys?"

Imani stared at the phone with a frown on her face, but she refused to lose her cool.

"Brandon, the last time I saw you, you were hugged up with your lil girlfriend, and I was strongly advised by the police officers to stay away from you. So, my question to you is, why in the hell are you texting me, if it's not about our boys?"

He took a deep breath before he spoke. "Imani, I'm so sorry. I screwed up. I want to apologize for being a jerk the past few months, and I want to show you that I've changed. I miss you, I miss our boys, and I miss our family. I made a huge mistake, and I'm willing to do whatever it takes to win you back."

Imani was caught off guard by his mea culpa. She hadn't heard anything remotely close to an apology or remorse in so long until she didn't know he still had it in him.

Brandon continued to plead his case, "My parents have their annual barbecue this weekend, and I really want you to be there. The boys are looking forward to seeing us both."

Imani listened as the contrition in his voice sounded sincere. But she was too afraid to trust him. He'd hurt her, and she couldn't easily dismiss the humiliation he'd put her through the past week. She couldn't seem to shake the image of him and that little girl. She thought of the new life she was making for the boys and herself and decided that she'd come too far, to throw it all away. She knew she was taking a risk, but to her, it was a risk she was willing to take.

She responded, "Brandon I've wasted four years of my life waiting for you to become my family. You were the one who took me for granted and stepped outside of the relationship in search of something better. I'm assuming it didn't work, so now you want to come crawling back. Well, I'm here to tell you, that it doesn't work like that. You have forced me to move on, and I'm really happy. Now I wish you the best, and I'll see you when you bring the boys back. Bye Brandon."

As Imani was in the process of ending the call, she could hear him yell "Wait!" But it was too late.

Brandon's call made her nervous. She lay there in bed trying to calm herself when her phone rang again. She hit ignore, and after the third call, he texted her.

"I will win you back. I won't ever give up on us."

She began to travel back down memory lane to the very beginning of their relationship. She remembered how kind, sweet, and considerate he was. That's the man he tried to portray himself as over the phone, but she wasn't completely convinced that he meant what he said. She quickly pushed those thoughts out of her mind. This was just a mind game he's playing. *Don't be fooled, keep moving forward with your plan.* She whispered to herself.

Imani began to shake once again, as she contemplated what to do next.

She stepped out of bed and began to pace about; she couldn't get back to sleep. She looked at the clock. It was close to three a.m. She decided to call LaShawn. She knew that there was a high possibility she'd be up.

There was loud music playing in the background when LaShawn answered the phone. "Hello. Imani. I can't hear you," LaShawn yelled into the phone.

Imani yelled back, "Hello. LaShawn. I can barely hear you as well." LaShawn said a few words, but it was no use. The only words Imani could make out were "after-hours club." Imani gently ended the call. *That girl never sits down.* Imani said to herself.

Imani resumed pacing the floor. She needed to talk to someone. Carlos was the only person who came to mind.

She made it up the flight of stairs and lightly tapped on his door. If he answered she'd go in, if he didn't she'd go back to her place and try and get some sleep.

In less than a minute he opened the door wearing pajama bottoms, a fresh white t-shirt, and slippers. He was wide-awake. He smiled once he saw her face. She smiled back as he welcomed her in.

She looked at him and said, “I can’t sleep.”

He looked at her and said, “Me either.”

He led her back to the music room. He sat there with the music turned very low as he watched old home movies of his wife and children.

Imani paused once she noticed what he was watching. “I’m sorry for interrupting, should I come back?”

He looked at her and said, “Not at all” as he patted the seat next to him. “I haven’t looked at these old movies since my wife has been gone.”

The movies had to have been over twenty years old, but the way he stared at the screen, made it seem as if it were only yesterday. His three beautiful young daughters all wore matching Cinderella dresses with tiara’s, and he and his beloved wore mouse ears. The Sanchez’s looked like a picture-perfect family.

Carlos pointed to his daughters on the screen, pausing the video on each daughter separately.

“This is my oldest daughter Marissa.” He smiled, pointing at the screen. “She’s an Engineer and has a husband and two children. They live in a huge house in Atlanta. Madison is the second oldest. She looks just like her mother.” He said proudly. “She’s a chemist with a husband and three children and they reside in Texas. This little beauty right here is my youngest daughter

Tina. She's a real estate agent who is married to the professional baseball player."

After he finished the introductions, he said, "I miss my daughters and the grandkids a lot. They each have been begging me to come to visit, but I haven't had the time."

Imani looked at Carlos with compassion and said, "please don't make that excuse. You own that bar, and you can shut it down anytime you feel like it. There's plenty of time."

Carlos let out a soft chuckle. "My daughters say the same thing."

Imani softly squeezed his hand. "I know it's hard to leave here without your wife, but you have to keep going."

Carlos' voice began to shake as he spoke, "Imani I know that I probably talk about Mary Ann a lot, but I can't help it. I miss her every single day. She was the rock of our family, and without her, I'm lost. That bar gives me, something to do and it takes my mind off of her."

Imani responded, "Well your girls need their father."

Carlos bowed his head. "I'd like to think that. However, I can never come close to their mother. It's just a special bond that women have. When Mary Ann was here, they came back home frequently. Since she's been gone, they hardly ever visit. It's just something about those mothers." He laughed nervously.

Imani just listened, as she thought of her father. She felt terrible for disappearing, and she planned to make it right real soon. She didn't ever want her father feeling like she loved or needed her mother more.

Carlos changed the subject. "Tell me something about your boys?" Imani perked up. She missed her boys and couldn't wait to see them in a few days.

"My boys are fraternal twins, and their names are Nelson Allen and Martin Peter Garrison. They're three years old, and one is a ball of fire, while the other one is calmer and laid back."

Mr. Sanchez said, "Well with names like that, they have to be special kids. I haven't heard those types of names since my generation. What is the origin of those names?"

Imani smiled because she was proud of her son's names. She was not surprised that he'd asked that question, as she had heard it often.

"Carlos, my boys are fraternal twins. Not only did they look very different, but their personalities were also different as well. Martin was born with a light complexion like his father, and he came out smiling. Nelson was born more of a dark brown like me, with a serious look on his face. The moment I laid my eyes on them, I said, I want my boys to be leaders. I understand how important names are. A name precedes you, and I didn't want my sons to have names where people could potentially prejudge them because of it. I chose to name them after great leaders, Nelson Mandela, and Martin Luther King Jr. Their middle names came from each of their grandfathers."

"That's very interesting. I knew you were a special lady the moment you walked into the bar and filled out the application. I'm fortunate to have gotten to know you." Carlos said.

Imani reached in and hugged him, for she felt like the lucky one.

Carlos sat back and stretched his arms as he continued to watch the old movies. Imani snuggled close under the pit of his arm and fell fast asleep.

Imani opened her eyes, and stared at the clock on the wall; it read six fifteen am. She was still snuggled in Carlos's arms, and she felt protected. She loved the fact that he never tried to take advantage of her vulnerability. He followed her lead, and she respected him more for that. Being so close to him gave her a sense of invincibility. Imani felt like she was sitting on top of the world. He took her mind off Brandon.

After a few minutes, she slipped from under his arms. He was sleeping so sound, that she didn't want to wake him. She grabbed the small blanket sitting on the chair and gently covered him with it. She kissed him on the cheek and whispered, "See you later on this evening," before she headed back down to her place.

Imani entered her bedroom and peeked at her cell phone. She was happy to find that there were no more missed calls from Brandon. She hoped he'd gotten the message. She had a new man in her life, and she couldn't be happier.

ଓ

It had been two days since Brandon last called, so Imani assumed he had gotten the message. She set her clothes out for the day and went over her schedule before heading to the shower. As the water washed over her body, she closed her eyes and gave thanks. Her life was peaceful.

Imani decided that it was time for her to stand up to her father. She could no longer prolong the inevitable. She was tired of running, hiding, sneaking, and lying. Carlos was her new man, and that was that. She was ready to show her parents what she'd accomplished on her own. If her parents couldn't accept it, then it was their loss. She had to grow up. She couldn't stay Peter McNair's little girl forever.

Imani reached inside her top drawer and counted her pay. She'd planned to close out the daycare bill, pick up some groceries, and visit her parents.

ଓ

As Imani turned onto her parents' street, she spotted Brandon's car sitting in front of their house. She contemplated stopping but quickly decided against it. *She didn't see the point.* She didn't care what Brandon said about her, or how much he apologized, their relationship was over.

Imani pulled off the block and headed over to LaShawn's place.

LaShawn was in her complexes parking lot with her trunk open and loading suitcases. Imani pulled up beside her car, jumped out and asked, "Hey girl, where are you going?"

LaShawn looked at Imani and smiled. "Girl we've both been so busy, we haven't had time to catch up. I hooked up with one of the designers at the fashion show, and she has invited me to Atlanta to help out with some of her designs. I couldn't pass on this opportunity, and I'll have my own room."

Imani smiled and gave her a big hug. "Oh, my goodness, that's awesome. Maybe Carlos and I can hop on a plane to come and check you out when you make it to the big leagues."

LaShawn gave Imani a sneer and said dryly. "Yeah, maybe you two could," before quickly changing the subject.

"Imani I thought you should know that Brandon stopped by the bar the other night. He looked so pitiful. I wanted to let him have it, but the look on his face told me there was no need to pile on. I didn't give up any information on your whereabouts, but the barmaid Jasmine did. She told him you were off. I told her she shouldn't have said anything."

Imani looked at LaShawn and said, "Girl, I don't care what he knows. Brandon is a boy. A child. And the only children that I have time for are my own. He's so far in my rearview mirror until I don't even see him anymore."

LaShawn gave Imani a perplexed look. "Well alright, Ms. lady. I guess you've got this all figured out."

Imani added, "I was going to go and see my parents, but I noticed Brandon's car was there. I have no idea what that was all about, and I don't even care. My heart is set on one person."

LaShawn looked at Imani while shaking her head. "You mean to tell me that you still haven't told your parents about Mr. Sanchez?"

"Well I was going to today, but they had company," Imani responded.

"Well, how do you think they're going to react?" LaShawn asked with a look of concern.

Imani rolled her eyes dismissively and said, "I don't care what they think, this is my life, and I'm going to live it the way I see fit. The only thing that Peter McNair runs is his mouth."

LaShawn suddenly stopped loading her bags and looked at Imani quizzically, "Well damn where is all of this coming from?"

Imani spoke with a newfound confidence; "My father doesn't believe that I'm capable of doing this on my own. I am a grown woman, and I don't need him anymore. He and Brandon were both holding me back. In just one week, I was able to acquire a nice home for my boys, a full time, well-paying job, a bank account, and a man who understands and appreciates me."

LaShawn looked at Imani with serious concern and pointed to her Jeep. "Imani, your father, might be a little overbearing but he has always been there for you. Look at what you're driving. I think you're a bit too hard on him."

Imani turned up her nose and said, "Are you talking about that piece of junk that I'm driving? The one where the engine light stays on, the oil leaks, and let's not talk about the buzz, squeaks, and rattles."

LaShawn's mouth fell wide open. She was mortified because she knew how hard Imani's father worked to get her that Jeep.

"Well, what if it doesn't work out with you and Mr. Sanchez?" LaShawn asked in a frustrated tone.

Imani was growing irritated. "LaShawn, I know what I am doing. Like I've said before, I'm dealing with a real man here. Trust me. It will work." Imani said adamantly.

LaShawn wasn't quite done. "I guess I'm playing Devil's Advocate here, but didn't you say that about Brandon?"

Imani huffed, as she was tired of being lectured, "This is different."

LaShawn wanted to keep going, but she could feel the tension brewing inside of them both. She'd given Imani enough to think about, so she let it go.

The ladies exchanged good-byes and Imani headed home. She needed to put her groceries away and take a nap before work.

Butterfly

The huge bouquet of red long-stemmed roses caught her eye the moment she stepped through the door. They sat behind the bar in a tall vase wrapped in gold and silver cellophane paper. The crowd was kind of thick as the "after-work affair" was in full swing. Hector walked over to Imani and pointed at the flowers. "The florist guy left those for you."

Imani was surprised; as she couldn't remember the last time she'd received flowers. If her memory served her correctly, it was after she had the twins when Brandon brought flowers to the hospital. Hector stood close by as she opened the card. Imani could feel him peering over her shoulder. She smiled as she pulled the card close to her chest.

"Well heck, I want to see who they're from too," Hector said as he walked away laughing.

Imani laughed back. "That's none of your business," although she did understand his curiosity. Since she'd started working with Carlos, a few people speculated that something was going on between the two, but she and Carlos never confirmed anything. They'd kept it professional in the presence of others. Since it had only been a little over a week, she knew it would only be a matter of time before the rumors would start swirling.

As she read the card, she smiled. "You are so beautiful. You deserve flowers every day XOXOXO."

Imani didn't have to guess who sent them. After the time they'd spent together the other evening, she believed that this was Carlos's way of saying that he was ready to take things to the next level. She felt warm and tingly on the inside as she thought of him. Carlos had done so much for her. He'd taken her places she'd never been, he made her feel special, treated her like the ultimate lady, and he taught her how to make it on her own.

Imani was also a bit nervous, but she knew the time had come for the two, to connect on a much deeper level. She believed that she was ready; however, she had her fears. "What if he changed after the intimacy? What if she didn't live up to his expectations?" Imani quickly pushed what she presumed were silly thoughts out of her head. Carlos was a real man. Real men don't play games. Real men know what they want. Of course, he wouldn't change. Carlos was like her King; her Knight in shining armor. He offered her a home, and not some two-bedroom apartment in his basement. This is what Imani had been waiting on; "a real man." She'd decided right then and there that she was willing to lay it all out on the line to make their relationship work.

Imani thought of her parents. She had to go and make it right with them. She knew that they wouldn't approve of her relationship right away, but once they saw that she had a stable home, a great job, and was able to care for herself and her children, they'd have no choice but to accept it. She figured that she and Brandon could be amicable when it came to parenting. Since both of their parents loved their grandchildren, they could be the bridge between she, Brandon and the children. They could pick up, and drop off the kids, at their homes and Brandon would never have to know where she lived. She was sad it had to be this way, but Brandon was the one who drew first blood by putting her out and stepping outside of their relationship. Besides, he was a boy, and there was no way in hell she'd go back to dating a boy.

Imani couldn't take her eyes off the beautiful flowers. She continued to stare and smell the roses. It was close to eight o'clock when Carlos finally walked through the door. He was dressed in a casual black suit, with black loafers wearing a fedora. Imani instantly thought of LaShawn teasing her. *"He's old enough to be your father."* Imani chuckled on the inside. I wonder how funny she will think it is when I'm her boss, and she's calling me Mrs. Sanchez.

Imani stood next to the flowers with a flirtatious smile as she walked over to greet him. Carlos looked surprised once he caught sight of the flowers. "Wow someone must think you're special." He said with a slight smile.

Imani played along with his little charade. She batted her eyes. "Well tonight we'll see just how special I am."

Carlos leaned in close so that he didn't have to shout over the music. "Imani I want to say thank you for the other evening. You are such a wonderful person, and I enjoyed your company. You have given me a new lease on life. Because of you, I am now ready to let go of the past, and start living and enjoying life again."

Imani let out a soft breath. She began to blush, "Carlos it's been my pleasure. I feel the same way too!"

Carlos clasped his hands and began to rub them together as he contemplated what to order. "Hmnnn I think I'll have a Jack and Coke." He said in an upbeat voice.

"Coming right up." She said in a tone that matched his.

As she served Carlos his drink, he handed her a twenty-dollar bill. He winked his eye and said, "Keep the change, pretty lady. We'll finish this discussion later." Imani was so enraptured by the smell of his cologne and the gentle words he'd spoken that she didn't get the chance to thank him for the tip and the flowers. Carlos had strolled off to the opposite side of the bar where his brother and a few older men accompanied him.

Imani felt good as she studied his body language. She could see the change in him. His look of quiet resignation, no longer present. He was giddy and effervescent. He'd seemed to switch from autopilot to full throttle. Carlos was happy.

Seeing Carlos happy made her happy. Imani was on a euphoric high as she continued to smell the roses. She couldn't help herself; they were beautiful. Things were looking up and falling right into place. Imani envisioned her and Carlos, getting married along the beach at some tropical Island with her boys right by her side. They'd vacation all over the country, she'd send the boys to the best schools, they'd dine at the finest restaurants, and maybe she'd even help LaShawn start up her business. Imani just loved this new life that she'd built.

Imani was in her own world, as she stared at Carlos while continuing to fantasize about their life together. She thought that maybe they could go car shopping tomorrow. She'd like to get rid of that old Jeep and upgrade to a newer one. The twins would love that. She thought to herself.

Imani was suddenly forced back into reality when the barmaid Jasmine, tapped her on the shoulder. Slightly embarrassed that she'd been caught daydreaming; Imani shifted her focus from Carlos to Jasmine. She bowed her head as Jasmine whispered in her ear.

"Imani, turn towards the door," Jasmine whispered in a panicked voice. Imani turned toward the door. "The guy that's walking thru the door is the one who was here looking for you the other night." Said Jasmine.

Imani slowly lifted her head. She paused. Her mouth flew open, and her heart sank. Imani gasped as the tall, lean, disheveled looking man was heading in her direction. He wore a black t-shirt with the words "Williams Construction" across the front of it, with worn out jeans, a black baseball cap, and a pair of dusty black work boots. He stopped directly in front of her and looked deep into her eyes. He didn't say a word for a few seconds. He just stared longingly at her.

Imani had found herself in a state of temporary paralyzes. Her entire body began to shake. It had been a little over a week since she'd last seen Brandon. However, as she looked at him, she noticed that he looked nothing like the cool, confident, young man she fell in love with five years ago. She almost felt sorry for him. His once polished appearance was gone. His face looked slimmer, his eyes were sunken, and his hair was untamed. She looked at him with pity.

Brandon finally spoke in a compassionate voice. "You really are beautiful. You really do deserve flowers every day."

Imani gasped and put her hand over her heart. She slowly turned to look at the roses. Her questioning eyes then shifted over to Carlos. Carlos hunched his shoulders, nodded his head and raised his glass. Imani let out a heavy breath as she turned back to Brandon. She was at a loss for words.

Jasmine noticed the weary look on Imani's face and said, "I'll cover for you."

Imani, still in disbelief said, "Thank You."

Imani was shaking as she slowly stepped from behind the bar and led Brandon over to a booth. She tried her best to sound angry, but she wasn't. She was confused. Although he looked nothing like himself, he was still handsome. She'd been so busy the entire week blocking him out until she never sat still to think of him. However, with him sitting right here in her face, she realized, she still loved him. She asked herself, "*Isn't love what got you here in the first place?"* Love was no longer enough.

Imani was afraid to travel back down the "love road" with Brandon. If she caved in, she might never have control over her life, and she may find herself homeless again. She couldn't let him back in. It was a setup, she was sure.

Imani furrowed her eyebrows and said, "Brandon what are you doing here?"

Brandon looked as though he were going to have a nervous breakdown. His eyes were red, he seemed tired, and his breathing was shallow.

"I came to win you back. Imani, I made a horrible mistake, and I'm paying dearly for it. I can't eat, I can't sleep, and I can't stop thinking about you. I've quit my job at Game Stop, and I picked up a new one at a construction company. I've been working myself to death so that I could make enough money to take care of my family on my own. Imani, please take me back."

Imani listened. She was now an emotional wreck. She wanted to believe him, but she was afraid. Afraid to trust, afraid to go backward, and afraid of giving up the new life she'd built. Imani was torn. Her eyes filled up with tears as she spoke. "Brandon, you can't just send flowers, and walk in here and profess your love for me, and expect for me to drop everything, and run off with you. Sending flowers doesn't make you a man. Sending flowers doesn't mean that you've changed. Poetic words have no meaning if there isn't any action behind them. How do I know you've changed?"

He looked at her and spoke with as much contrition as he could, "Imani, I've learned a lot this past week. I tried talking to my mother about us, and she told me that I was not man enough for you. When she told me that she told you to move on; that hurt me. It didn't hurt me because she said that, it hurt me because it was true. I knew if I ever wanted to get you back, I'd have to be a man, and do what grown men do, so I sent flowers. I figured that was a good start. When I spotted you from the door, I saw you smell them and smile. This past week I've been longing to see your smile."

Imani sat there not knowing what to do. She then said, “Why couldn’t you be this Brandon when we were together? Why did it take for me to move on to see this side of you? This tells me that every time I want to see this side, I will have to pack up and leave. Well, Brandon, that’s too much packing. I’m settled right now, and pretty comfortable.”

Brandon was afraid. Nothing he said seemed to be working, but he continued to plead, “Imani I am a man!” He said assuredly. “But I can’t prove that to you if you won’t let me.

Imani sat there and gave a blank stare.

Brandon’s eyes suddenly began to fill with water. He took several deep breaths and stared her dead in the eyes and spoke somberly, “I also understand that a man has to accept responsibility for his actions and deal with the consequences. Imani I came here a few days ago looking for you and you weren’t here.” Brandon huffed before looking away for several seconds. “Imani, I don’t care where you’ve been, or what you’ve done. I just want you back.” A tear fell from his eye as he extended his hands reaching for her. Imani never reached back.

Brandon was desperate. He was losing ground. He took his eyes off Imani and focused his attention across the room. He let out a heavy sigh and somberly nodded his head in the direction of Mr. Sanchez. “Imani if you look me straight in the eyes and tell me that you honestly don't want me and that you want to be with that old man over there, I'll leave!"

Imani paused. She became numb. *He knew.* She slowly turned, until her eyes landed on Carlos. He seemed to pay them both no minds as he continued to laugh and drink with his buddies.

She turned her attention back to Brandon. Tears fell freely from her eyes. She was angry. She didn't bother to ask how he knew, that was irrelevant. Brandon was the reason they were here. He did this. He pushed her away. Now he just thought some sad song could fix it. Well, it wasn't that easy.

Brandon continued to reach for her as he pleaded one last time. "Tell me you want me to leave Imani. Tell me that you really want to be with that old man. Just say it."

Imani couldn't say it, and she couldn't hold his hands either. Instead, she abruptly rose from the table. Brandon's head then collapsed on the table. She rushed behind the bar to grab her purse.

She looked at the Jasmine and said, "Please take over for me, and you can have my tips." Jasmine tried asking if everything was ok, but Imani didn't respond.

Imani looked over at Carlos one last time. He began to rise from his seat in an attempt to reach out to her. She halted him by throwing her hand up.

When Imani made it to her Jeep, she started the engine and pulled off. The minute she made it out the parking lot, she started bawling. She bawled so hard that she could hardly drive.

She understood that this was more than about what she wanted. She and Brandon had children, and their children deserved to be happy. She had prepared a home for them, and she believed they'd be happy there. Brandon forced her to be this way. Him putting her out was like a kick in the stomach, and she didn't ever want to feel that again. She didn't trust him.

She pulled up to her home and ran inside. She paused the moment she'd shut the door. Imani just stared at her home, admiring its beauty. She lingered through the house touching the pillows, the picture frames, placemats, floral arrangements, and the throw rugs. She just loved the place.

Imani picked up her cell phone and went into the kids' room. The two toddler beds were neatly made with blue and red comforters, matching lamps, tables, and rugs. *The kids are going to love their new home.* Imani whispered to herself. She sat on the edge of one of the beds and just stared at the floor. She didn't want to leave all of this. Imani began to weep.

Imani needed to talk to someone. She dialed the only person who could help her make sense of this entire situation. LaShawn was in Atlanta probably having the time of her life, but Imani needed her. She hoped and prayed she could talk.

LaShawn answered right away. Imani was surprised that there was no loud music, voices, or background noise; it was complete silence.

"Hello Imani," LaShawn answered in a sleepy voice.

"Hello, LaShawn how is it going?" Imani replied in a trembling voice, trying her best to hold back the tears.

LaShawn could detect something was wrong right away, so she spoke with caution. "Imani, I'm a little tired, but I'm fine. Hey, aren't you supposed to be at work?" She asked in a concerned voice.

Imani suddenly couldn't hold back any longer. She burst into tears.

LaShawn gasped loudly into the phone. "Oh, my goodness Imani. What's wrong? Why are you crying?"

Imani tried to pull it together, but instead, she stuttered over her words. "I. Needed. To. Talk. To. Someone…"

LaShawn interrupted her. "Slow down. Breathe. I can't understand a word you're saying."

Imani slowed down her breathing. She caught her breath and began to speak.

"LaShawn, I'm just a mess right now. Brandon knows about Carlos and me. He's been calling me and begging me to come back to him. He sent flowers to the bar, and then he showed up pleading with me to take him back. I'm just so confused right now. He sent me through a lot. Now he wants to disrupt the new life I've built for the boys and myself. I can't trust him."

Imani sat there waiting for a response, but the phone became silent.

"Hello LaShawn, are you there?" Said Imani.

"Yes, I'm listening." Said LaShawn.

"Well, what do you think?" Imani asked.

LaShawn sighed and hesitated for several seconds before she spoke. Her tone was calm and measured, "Imani have you ever just sat back and asked yourself what role you played in all this?"

Imani whimpered. "I mean I tried. I tried really hard. I was a great mother, girlfriend and college student. You know this LaShawn."

LaShawn replied, "Well, to be honest, I don't think you're being totally fair to Brandon."

"What? Oh, so now you're on his side?" Imani snarled.

"Imani!" LaShawn yelled. "This isn't about sides. It's about fairness, and right now I believe you are being unfair to Brandon. You must give that man some credit. He tried too."

LaShawn went on to defend her statement...

"Imani since we were young girls, you've always acted much older than you were. You never really dated anyone, because you said boys were so immature. When you told me you had a real boyfriend, I was so excited for you. When you finally introduced us, I couldn't give him thumbs up, or thumbs down, because you were pregnant. If it hadn't been for his father, you would have been married at nineteen. You two didn't get a chance to know each other."

Imani was becoming frustrated. "That's not fair; you're blaming this entire situation on me."

LaShawn huffed. "Imani, I'm not blaming all of this on you. What I'm saying is that at least he tried. At least he didn't take off, and run like so many other men would have. He brought you into his parents' home, and you two had a good life. As far as the pregnancy… well you have complete control over your body. You could have taken the necessary precautions to prevent that."

Imani shot back, "That's why I don't want to go back and take that chance. Brandon put me out! Now I have busted my butt, building this life and I'm not just going to let him come in and mess it up!"

After Imani said that, the phone grew silent again. Imani thought LaShawn had ended the call, so she called her name. "LaShawn? Are you still there?"

LaShawn took a deep breath and let out a long sigh. "Imani, are you listening to yourself?" She yelled.

"What is that supposed to mean?" Imani yelled back.

LaShawn said, "As your friend, my job is to tell you the truth. If I didn't tell you the truth, then I wouldn't be your friend. Now with that being said, you and Brandon haven't done a goddamn thing but take Shortcuts! His parents, as well as your parents, have been propping you both up. You two haven't done anything on your own. As far as you and Mr. Sanchez, that's not even real. It's not sustainable. Imani, you haven't even put in any real work. Mr. Sanchez is a nice, generous, but lonely man, who felt sorry for you and you saw that as an opportunity to move to the front of the line. Now you somehow mistake this as hard work, or you *busting* your butt. Well, girlfriend, you got it all wrong."

Imani became quiet. Her feelings were hurt as LaShawn was just getting started.

"Imani, if you want to know the definition of busting your butt, then I suggest you take a look at my life. I've been doing this for quite a while. I left home as soon as I graduated from high school because my mother and grandmother were hoarders. I didn't want to live like that, so I had to pave my own way. I guess I was blessed with the gift of creativity so that I could make a good life for myself because school and I weren't exactly the best of friends."

Imani was feeling low, but she finally spoke. "LaShawn, I don't know what to say. I never thought of Brandon and myself as taking shortcuts. As far as your life, I admire you and always have. I've never had the chance to experience the fun, carefree, life you have, but these last two weeks have given me a glimpse, and I enjoyed it."

LaShawn let out a laugh. "Ha! Fun? Care Free? A glimpse?" she repeated.

"Imani, you don't know the half of what I go through or what I've been through. On the surface, I appear happy, but deep down inside I am not. I am so tired of doing this on my own but what choice do I have? I'd love to have a solid relationship or a man to sweep me off my feet and carry some of this load, but I don't have that. I run myself ragged so that I can stay busy and not think about my sad life. Imani, there are twenty-four hours in a day, and I have to find a way to fill each and every minute of the day. I never tell anyone this, but sometimes when the party is over, and the lights turn off, and I'm home all alone I cry! That's right you heard me, I freaking cry!"

Imani felt bad. She didn't understand. "LaShawn, why do you cry? You have what most women dream of having, and you're beautiful on top of that."

LaShawn responded, "Money and beauty don't mean a thing when you don't have anyone to share it with."

Imani took a deep breath. "Oh LaShawn, I'm so sorry. I had no idea."

LaShawn replied, "Please don't feel sorry for me. I'm ok and just because my prince hasn't arrived, doesn't mean he's not on the way. In the meantime, I am going to consider volunteering at the animal shelter, or I may even consider becoming a foster parent. There's plenty of love to go around. This world is too big, with too many people, for anyone to be alone. I don't believe anyone is meant to be alone." Now, enough about my life, let's get back to you.

LaShawn finally softened her tone.

"Imani, I need for you to go and pack your things and get out of Mr. Sanchez's house. You've had your fun this past week; now it's time for you to get back to reality. Living under the same roof with a man that's old enough to be your father isn't reality. You're cheating yourself and your children. Mr. Sanchez and his late wife raised their children, and I believe you and Brandon should do the same. Brandon, in spite of all of his flaws, is a good man, who loves you. I could tell by the pitiful look on his face the other night when he came to the bar. Now you and Brandon both need to go to the back of the line and start all over; no more taking the easy way out. You two need to figure this thing called life out on your own. You've both experienced other people so that should be behind you both. Now it's time for you two to go and build something together without all of the distractions. Those wonderful boys deserve that." said LaShawn.

The phone became silent.

"Imani, are you still there?" LaShawn said.

Imani responded with a bit of sadness in her voice. "Yes, I'm here, and I am listening."

LaShawn closed with, "Well I just want you to know that I'll be in the background rooting for you and Brandon."

Imani wiped the tears that were forming in her eyes and whispered, "I have so much to think about. Thank you for being my best friend and putting up with me."

LaShawn closed with, "You're welcome. That's what true friends are for. Now, I'm hanging up this phone because I need to get some rest. Imani, I'm tired. I love you, and I'll talk to you soon." LaShawn then ended the call.

ᘓ

Imani walked through the house once more before heading to the kitchen. She reached under the counter and grabbed several garbage bags. She let out a tear-ful laugh and said to herself, *"I have to put luggage on my list."*

Imani began tossing the throw pillows into the bags when there was a light tapping on her door.

"Imani, it's Carlos. I just wanted to make sure you're ok."

Imani took the back of her hand and tried to wipe away any traces of tears. She made several small faint breaths before opening the door. She had never been so torn before in her entire life, but she was sure of her decision.

Carlos stood in the doorway with a faint smile on his face. She welcomed him in. He spotted the bags, and he knew she was leaving. Imani started to speak first, but he interrupted.

"You don't have to explain yourself, pretty lady, I witnessed it with my own two eyes. You and that young man have some unfinished business, and I would be a selfish man if I came between that. I know that look. I was once that same foolish young man. I almost lost Mary Ann early in our relationship, because I took too long to commit. I thought she'd always be there, so I took her for granted. When she finally took me back, I never took her for granted again. I was so scared of her leaving again that I immediately took her down to the courthouse, to make sure she wouldn't get away."

Imani and Carlos both laughed as he finished speaking.

"What that young man did this evening, took guts and courage. He's a fighter and not a quitter. You have to understand that you'll never know how strong your love is for a person until it's been tested. Imani, you and that young man have been apart for almost two weeks. I believe that's as big of a test that any relationship can take. Imani, seeing you and that gentleman this evening, let me know that you both are capable of passing that test."

Imani began to blush as Carlos finished.

"Imani I can't say that I won't miss you, because I will. However, I'm wise enough to know that you were sent to me for a reason." Carlos let out a chuckle, "I really believe Mary Ann sent you. She wants me to get back out there and live my life. Thanks to you Imani I know I can do it. These have been some of the best days of my life, and I just can't put a price tag on it. You gave me laughter, companionship as well friendship and I am forever grateful. You will always hold a special place in my heart."

He then said, "Imani I plan to travel soon. If you decide that you don't want to go, your job is still open, and this place is still available."

When Carlos offered her the job and his home, her heart nearly melted. However, she heard and understood LaShawn's words loud and clear. *"It wasn't real. It wasn't hers."*

Imani looked at Carlos and said "Thank you, but Carlos I have to do this all on my own. Struggle teaches more than pleasure ever could." When she said that, he smiled.

Imani added, "This has certainly been a week I'll never forget. It's been an adventure worth taking. My entire life I've witnessed my father treat my mother like a real lady. I've always wanted someone to treat me like that. Carlos, that's one of the greatest things that I'll take away from our journey. I not only witnessed what a lady should be treated like; I also had the chance to feel it. It happens to be one of the greatest feelings in the world. Because of you, I was able to experience what having my own would feel like, and it's a wonderful feeling. I've learned from you that it's no longer about words. They're cheap. It's about action. It speaks."

Carlos stood there speechless. Imani thought that she saw his eyes water, But before any tears could fall, she wrapped her arms around his waist and just held him. He held her back. She sure was going to miss him, but she knew that their season had come to an end.

☙

The home was quiet and dark. Imani rang the doorbell hoping they'd answer. The last time she'd spoken with her father, he told her to stay away.

Her father peeked through the window. He took one look at his daughter's face and snatched the door open. Imani stood there tired and exhausted. Her father let out a heavy sigh, opened his arms, and welcomed her in. He didn't say one word. He just held his daughter tight, like he was holding her for the very first time.

Discussion Questions

1. Describe how you felt about Imani at the beginning of the story? Did your views change toward the end?

2. Did you have a favorite character? Who and Why?

3. What relevance did Peter McNair's background have to the story?

4. Do you think that LaShawn was a good friend? Why or why not?

5. "The desire to stand out should be much greater than the desire to fit in." Please describe in your own words, what this quote means to you.

6. Explain Brandon's greatest strengths and weaknesses?

7. Explain Carlos Sanchez's greatest strength and weaknesses?

8. Do you believe that Imani's actions were justified at the Game Stop?

9. At the end of the story, Imani was left with four main options. In your opinion, which was the most logical option and why?

10. Can you explain in your own words what Shortcuts mean to you?

11. Can you give both the Pro's and Con's of taking Shortcuts?

About the Author

T. L. Criswell is an author and a poet. Her creative writing style gives life to her belief that what you put out into the universe determine your destiny. She is passionate about living a happy and well-balanced life, which is reflective in her writings, often described as authentic, witty, humorous, and poignant. With an inspired desire for self-expression, Criswell is a spiritual person, as well as a freethinker who has been writing poetry and short stories since she was a young girl.

T.L. Criswell is grateful for her mentor Ben C. Smith for helping her to find her literary voice in 2012.

In 2018, the Detroit Library picked up her debut novel ***"The Peacemaker,"*** a book about stolen opportunities and redemption. The Library purchased 900 copies for DPS students and selected Ms. Criswell as the featured author for their annual author day, a 2-day event. Her follow-up novel Peace on That: The Peacemaker II also tackles common life issues.

Shortcuts: Choices and Consequences, is her third published novel and she also has published two short stories.

T.L. Criswell resides in the Detroit Metropolitan area with her husband and her son.

Made in the USA
Middletown, DE
17 August 2019